Hornet Heaven

Volume 2

Olly Wicken

Hornet Heaven is the paradise where Watford fans go in the afterlife. It turns out we're not just Watford 'til we die, we're Watford for all eternity.

In Hornet Heaven, you can watch all Watford's matches for the rest of time. You can also re-visit any Watford match in history, time and time again.

It's to die for.

The Hornet Heaven stories are dedicated to everyone who has ever loved Watford Football Club.

CONTENTS

Acknowledgements

1 The Great Man Is Gone   1

2 Deconstructing Harry   27

3 Up For The Cup   43

4 Not Quite Managing   52

5 Fanzines Are Bad For You   77

6 Boring Boring Watford   84

7 Going Backwards   101

8 A World Without Beauty   126

9 One Man Alone   149

10 The Tribute   183

11 The Plastic   222

12 Never Too High, Never Too Low   246

13 Divided Loyalties   279

ACKNOWLEDGEMENTS

Warm thanks to the Watford fans who helped bring the Hornet Heaven stories into being. In particular:

Watford fans Colin Mace and Jon Moonie whose voice and radio production talents turned the stories into an award-winning podcast.

Watford fan Mike Smart who co-wrote the story 'The Great Man Is Gone'.

Watford fan Ed Wicken who co-wrote the story 'Never Too High, Never Too Low'.

Watford fan Andy Barker who created the logo.

Watford fans Geoff Wicken and David Harrison who helped improve each story.

Watford fan Lionel Birnie who commissioned the original Hornet Heaven story 'Only Till I Die?' for Volume 2 of the Tales From The Vicarage series of books.

Watford fans Oliver Phillips and Trefor Jones who assembled the historical facts on which the stories are built.

Watford fans Alan and Margaret Wicken who first took me to Vicarage Road on September 7th 1968.

You Horns.

Olly Wicken
October 2018

1

THE GREAT MAN IS GONE

EARTH SEASON 1987/88

Sitting high in the main stand at Vicarage Road, Henry Grover — the man who founded Watford Rovers in 1881 — leaned back and sighed. He said: 'You know, Johnny, the club just won't be the same now that Graham Taylor isn't around.'

Johnny Allgood — Watford's first-ever boss from 1903 to 1910 — was sitting with Henry.

'Aye,' he agreed sadly.

Henry continued: 'The truth is, he was by far our greatest ever manager. There won't be another like GT for the whole of eternity.'

'Very true,' Johnny agreed again, glancing down at

the new boss in Taylor's place on the bench.

'But something tells me we'll be remembering his successor for a very long time too,' Johnny said solemnly. 'Dave Bassett will have a huge and immediate impact on this club.'

'Oh good!' Henry replied enthusiastically. 'Splendid! This season is going to be marvellous!'

* * *

In Hornet Heaven, on August 15th 1987, an elderly man stood with an elderly woman on the crowded Family Terrace. It was Watford's first match after Graham Taylor had departed.

A certain sadness seemed to hover over the terrace. There was also an air of unease about whether the new people in charge would carry on doing things in the same way as Taylor.

But the pair of elderly fans were bothered by a more immediate concern.

'Oh dear, I can't see Tom and Mark anywhere,' said a fan called Neville Simpson who'd died a year earlier — in 1986.

'They have to be here,' Florence Simpson insisted.

'It's the first day of the season. And everyone needs to rally round now that GT isn't with us anymore. Go and search again.'

'Maybe Tom and Mark are on holiday,' Neville said. 'People in the land of the living do have other things to do, you know. '

'Only lightweights have other things to do when Watford are playing at home,' Florence said firmly. 'And no member of this family, living or dead, has any business being a lightweight. Go and find Tom and Mark. Go on. Do what I say, child.'

Neville rolled his eyes at Florence. 'I'm not a child, mother,' he said. 'I was 72 when I died.'

'Well, you're behaving like a particularly daft child if you think it's at all acceptable that two descendants of mine might be missing a home game. We're a Watford family. Always have been, always will be.'

'You're over-reacting, mother. Cut them some slack. If Tom and Mark aren't here, it's bound to be for a good reason.'

'Goodness, child. You need to change your attitude. It's as sloppy as this Trevor Senior's close control. I'm beginning to think that the reason your son and grandson aren't here is precisely because they've inherited your lackadaisical approach to life.'

'Honestly, mother! There'll have been events beyond their control. Anything could have happened to them...'

Neville paused for a moment.

'Oh no,' he said.

'What?' Florence asked.

'Maybe… maybe they're not out there in the land of the living because…'

Neville turned and headed back to the ancient turnstile. He said: 'I need to find out.'

Florence called after him: 'Stop! Where are you going? You can't miss a Watford game! You're disgracing the family! Come back!'

* * *

Neville emerged from the ancient turnstile onto Occupation Road. Normally, he would have turned left up the slope towards the programme hut, but this time Neville turned right and walked down the pot-holed road past the grubby garages.

After a few yards, he found himself going from the eternal sunshine of Hornet Heaven into the ashen half-light of the limbo where new arrivals materialised. He whispered to himself: 'Please don't let them be here. Not yet. Please.'

Neville stopped and waited anxiously in the gloom. He wanted to speak to Lamper — Hornet Heaven's chief steward — a former hooligan — whose job it was to meet all new residents as they arrived.

Soon he heard footsteps behind him.

But it wasn't Lamper. It was Florence.

'There you are, child.'

'Mother! You're missing the match. I thought you said—'

'I'm permitting myself to watch it later. I've come to help you find Tom and Mark. It'll be super if they're in Hornet Heaven already.'

'Super? It'll be terrible. Tom's only 43. Mark's only 12. They're far too young.'

'Being in Hornet Heaven will be good for them. No distractions. They'll never miss another Watford game. No disgracing the family.'

'You're actually wishing them dead? How could you? Tom and Mark have got long lives ahead of them on earth. Their lives go far beyond just watching Watford. They've got richer, more varied lives than that—'

Suddenly, a loud voice interrupted Neville: 'Oi! What's going on 'ere?'

Neville and his mother turned to see the snarling face of Lamper, the steward, leering at them through the twilight.

'You ain't allowed down here,' Lamper said, relishing the prospect of conflict. 'Want some, do ya?'

'No, not at all, Lamper,' Neville said defensively. 'We just need to speak to you.'

'Oh,' Lamper said, disappointed. 'Bollocks. You see, now Taylor's gone, I was hoping we could drop all this community togetherness rubbish and get a massive ruck going. Good old knuckle. Like you don't get on the Family bleeding Terrace what Mr Goody-Goody Graham Taylor brought in.'

Florence pushed her son aside.

'How dare you, steward? How dare you disrespect Mr Taylor's legacy to this club, you ugly yob!'

Lamper grinned.

'This is more like it!' he said. 'Bring it on, you horrid old hag!'

Lamper and Florence moved menacingly towards each other. Neville jumped between them to separate them.

'Calm down, both of you,' he said. 'This isn't the right time. We're here because something terrible may have happened.'

Lamper and Florence backed away from each other, scowling.

Neville explained: 'We need to know whether my son and grandson, Tom and Mark, have recently arrived in Hornet Heaven. They're younger generation.'

'Ooh, like a scrap, do they?' Lamper asked optimistically.

'Please just answer the question. Have they arrived?

'Nah. They ain't.'

'Oh, thank God,' Neville breathed heavily. 'Thank God. I want to spend eternity with them, but not yet.'

As Lamper skulked off back into the shadows, Neville said to his mother: 'I'm so relieved, mother. They're still alive!'

'Well, I'm not relieved. If they haven't died, they've got no good reason for missing a home game. It's shocking.'

'Mother, that's not—'

'You've let your son and grandson get out of control. You need to fix things. The integrity of this family depends on it.'

Briskly, Florence turned and headed up the slope — out of the dusk and back towards the brightness of Hornet Heaven.

Neville stood in the gloom and watched his mother go. She wasn't normally as bad as this. He couldn't work out what had got into her. If anything needed fixing, he reckoned, it was Florence Simpson.

*   *   *

Three days later, Neville bumped into Johnny Allgood in the programme hut. Johnny had been renowned as an astute tactician down on earth, so Neville asked him for advice.

'I don't know what to do about mother,' Neville said. 'Her views have suddenly become more extreme — on loyalty to Watford; on loyalty to the family.'

'Aye, we're seeing a lot of this at the moment,' Johnny replied. 'It's a grief reaction.'

'Grief? But we haven't suffered a family loss.'

'Ah, but we have. We all have. Graham Taylor has gone. Emotionally, it's a lot for people to cope with. Everybody loved him. More than they realised.'

'But GT's only gone to Villa. And we've got Dave Bassett now. He won his first match. He's a straight replacement, isn't he?'

'Well, that's an interesting question. Can GT ever be replaced? He transformed this club. He gave it a meaning in our lives that it never had before.'

'That's true, but—'

'You see, your mother's reaction suggests to me that she's unsettled at Graham's going. At this time of change, she's clinging to what she knows. Watford and family have become more important to her than ever.'

Neville thought about this. What Johnny was saying made a lot of sense.

Suddenly someone called out from the back of the hut: 'Programme's in!'

Johnny fetched two copies of that evening's game at Nottingham Forest and handed them to Neville. Johnny said: 'Take her to the City Ground, Neville. And look after her.'

*   *   *

Neville and Florence stood in the away section at Nottingham Forest and watched Dave Bassett's second match in charge. Watford lost 1-0 under the floodlights. Something seemed to be missing about the performance.

At the final whistle, Neville suddenly saw Tom and Mark on the terrace. He was amazed. He hadn't bothered looking out for them because Tom and Mark never normally travelled to away games.

'Mother! Look! There they are!'

'At an away game! Marvellous, child! They're Watford after all! It's in their blood!'

The two of them rushed over to be close to Tom and Mark. With difficulty, they managed to contain their joy and excitement so that they could eavesdrop on the two living Simpsons.

They heard Mark say: 'Away games are rubbish, Dad!'

Florence laughed indulgently. She said: 'Ahhh! Sweet boy! In this family, when you're Watford through and through, rubbish games simply aren't a problem! You just stick with the club.'

In the land of the living, Mark's father Tom said: 'Away games weren't so rubbish under Graham Taylor. We always gave them much more of a go. But I guess we're going to have to get used to them, lad, given that we won't be going to many more home games.'

Neville and Florence turned to each other.

Florence shrieked: 'What?! That's completely unacceptable! They've got all the loyalty of… of… Mo Johnston!'

'Sshh, mother!' Neville said. 'We need to know more.'

Tom said to his son: 'At least we haven't got as long a journey home as the other Watford fans. At this time of night, it's only an hour back to Birmingham.'

'They've moved to Birmingham?' Florence cried. 'But we're a Watford family!'

Florence made a noise Neville had never heard her make before. She covered her face with her hands.

Neville put a hand on his mother's shoulder.

She shrugged it off and marched back towards the ancient turnstile, tears streaming.

* * *

When Neville arrived back on Occupation Road, he tried to work out why Tom and Mark would have moved to Birmingham. He half-wondered if they'd loved Graham Taylor so much that they'd followed him there — now that The Great Man was at Villa. Neville dismissed the thought. GT was indeed a great man, but football fans' loyalties always remained attached to a club despite changes in personnel. Didn't they?

Neville walked up the slope and found his mother. She was sitting on the step of the Red Lion pub. She looked inconsolable. He sat down beside her.

'Everything's fallen apart,' she said. 'Ever since we lost GT. Nothing will ever be the same again.'

Neville took his mother's hand. They sat in silence for a while.

Then Florence said: 'I'm starting to feel my season ticket has no value anymore.'

At first, Neville didn't understand. No-one in Hornet Heaven had season tickets. They had programmes instead.

'You did keep my season ticket, didn't you?' she asked.

Now Neville realised what his mother was talking about. She meant her first season ticket — from 1920/21. It had been small, slim, and blue — like a tiny hardback book without pages. The outside was embossed. The inside stated that it admitted her to the ground and stand at Cassio Road.

Neville said: 'Of course I kept it, mother.'

The season ticket had been something of an heirloom in their family. Florence had left it to Neville when she died in 1948. Unfortunately, his own recent death had been sudden — and he had no idea what would have happened to the season ticket since. So he moved the conversation on.

He said: 'I'm sure Tom and Mark still love the club, mother.'

Florence looked at him through her tears. Neville could tell there was something she was finding it difficult to say.

Eventually she found the strength to say it.

'I hope they still love the club,' she whispered. 'It's just that… without GT around the place any more… I'm not sure I can.'

Florence gulped back a deep sob. She wept.

Neville sat with her, in the doorway of the Red Lion, and held her.

* * *

Over the next few weeks, Florence's sorrow turned to anger. Bassett sold Taylor's last ever signing, Richard Hill. Then Bassett sold one of the stars of Taylor's last season, David Bardsley. The season wasn't going well. Watford had won only two league games by the end of September.

On October 3rd, in the programme hut, Neville handed Florence a programme to the away game at Coventry. His mother was at breaking point.

'No,' she said. 'I don't want to go. Bassett's destroying our club, game by game. I don't want to witness it.'

'But it's an away game near Birmingham,' Neville said. 'Tom and Mark should be there. You want to see your family, don't you? That'll cheer you up.'

'No, it won't. The club isn't the same — and Tom and Mark aren't the same. They've betrayed us. They've become long-distance fans.'

'Steady on, there's nothing wrong with—'

'Long-distance fans have no commitment.'

'Mother, that's not—'

'No passion.'

'You're generalising, Mother. They—'

'They're not proper Watford people!'

Florence was barely holding herself together. Neville took her gently by the hand.

Florence looked down at his hand and nodded. Her

son was probably right. Seeing her loved ones would make her feel better.

She let him lead her towards the ancient turnstile.

* * *

As soon as they took their places in the away end at Highfield Road, Neville saw what he wanted to see. He said brightly: 'There we are, Mother! There's Tom!'

Florence peered across. 'But where's young Mark?'

They went over and stood next to Tom. Mark was nowhere to be seen.

'Well, that's it, then,' Florence said. 'He's lost.'

'Oh, Mother. We haven't even started looking for him yet.'

'Lost to the club, I mean. Lost to the family.'

The words hit Neville hard. He knew that young Mark was in his formative years as a football fan. The boy's absence was a bad sign.

'I'm sure he isn't lost,' Neville said, trying to convince himself as much as his mother. 'Let me go and look for him.'

Neville searched the away terrace from side to side. He was just about to give up when he heard Mark's voice. His heart lifted.

He turned, smiling, in the direction Mark's voice had come from. He found he was looking into the next section along. He frowned. This was the home section. Now he spotted Mark standing with a group of boys — school-friends from the West Midlands presumably — who were wearing light blue scarves. Mark was laughing and joking with them, clearly part of the group.

The shock hit Neville like a hammer blow. His grandson was now a Coventry fan.

He felt dazed. He found himself staggering down the terrace. Then he found himself on the pitch in Coventry's penalty area. A Gary Porter through-ball — which the lumbering Trevor Senior completely missed — rolled into Neville's path. Neville could have put Watford into the lead if he hadn't been dazed, dead and — marginally — offside.

Instead, he collapsed to the turf — as comprehensively as Watford Football Club were collapsing in Graham Taylor's absence.

* * *

Neville became aware of his mother helping him to his

feet.

'My darling son!' she cried. 'Are you alright? I was so worried. You went down like Albert McClenaghan taking a throw-in.'

Neville looked around at the crowd of 16,000 real-world people. He knew they couldn't see him, but he still felt humiliated.

'This is all Tom's fault,' he said, and marched back into the away section to confront his son.

Tom was reading the programme, completely oblivious to his father, but that didn't stop Neville. He said: 'This has gone far enough, Tom! My mother made sure her son was a Hornet. I made sure my son was a Hornet. You have to make sure your son is a Hornet. Being a Watford family is all about continuity.'

Tom looked up and glanced at the pitch. He yelled: 'Come on, Senior! My dad could run faster than that!'

Neville was flattered to hear he was still in his son's thoughts. But he wasn't to be deterred. He continued: 'Listen to me, son. You have to find a way to show Mark what it means to be a Watford fan. I know Taylor's gone. I know Bassett's wrecking the place. But what Taylor built was so good, it can't be destroyed. It mustn't be destroyed. It needs to be carried on for generations.'

Neville paused. For a moment, Tom had a wistful look in his eye. Almost as if he'd heard his father.

But he hadn't heard his father. He'd just seen Tony Agana go on a mazy run and dribble the ball into touch.

Tom went back to reading his programme. Neville felt powerless. At the end of Watford's latest defeat, he watched Tom make his way to the exit. He called after him: 'Please, son. Talk to your boy. Show him what Watford means to you. To all of us. Do whatever it takes. Keep our Watford family together.'

But Tom didn't hear Neville — and disappeared back home to Birmingham.

* * *

More defeats followed under Dave Bassett's management. By December, Watford were in the relegation zone with just three wins since the opening day of the season.

On December 12th, Neville and Florence went to the 1-0 home defeat against Luton Town. It was especially painful. They were glad that Tom and Mark weren't there to see it.

But one of the conversations they overheard on the Family Terrace did make them feel a little better.

'Blimey,' a fan said, staring bleakly at the pitch, 'I wouldn't go to the end of my road to watch this rubbish.'

'Speak for yourself, mate,' said a man with a strong twang to his accent. 'I've travelled a bit further than that.'

'Christ! You haven't come all the way from Australia, have you? You poor bugger.'

'Brisbane, mate,' the Aussie said. '30 hours of travel.'

Florence turned to Neville in amazement. She said: 'That's long-distance.'

'Just to see the mighty Horns, mate,' the Aussie said.

'That's commitment,' Florence said.

'I've been looking forward to this for three years since I last came,' the Aussie added. 'Every single day. Couldn't wait to be at Vicarage Road again. And you know what? Despite what's happening on the pitch, I can't wait for my next trip either.'

'That's passion,' Florence said.

Neville raised a smile. And even though Watford lost to the filthy Hatters, both Neville and Florence left the ground feeling a little more hopeful that their descendants, no matter how far-flung, would always keep Watford in their hearts.

* * *

Over the next three weeks, things got worse. The defeats continued. More symbolically, though, Bassett dropped Tony Coton — the winner of the Player Of The Season award for both of the last two seasons of Graham Taylor's reign, and arguably The Great Man's finest ever purchase.

In early January 1988, Florence sat down in the Supporters' Club bar with Henry Grover, the man who founded Watford Rovers in 1881. She wanted him to take action over the crisis, but the Father Of The Club seemed distracted.

'Why aren't you listening to me, Mr Grover?'

'Mmm? Sorry. I do beg your pardon.'

'Why are you gazing at the wall?'

'Ah. I was just admiring the paint effect on the new wallpaper. Rag-rolling, I think it's called. Very 1988. And so effective in soft pastel shades. Quite sublime.'

'Shut up and listen to me. You're our leader. You

need to intervene to save the club from Dave Bassett. All Graham Taylor's good work is being undone. My future descendants are in danger of not being Watford fans. I won't have it.'

'I see. Well, I genuinely wish I could intervene. People have been requesting it for years — even when Graham Taylor was here. Last season, Skilly Williams begged me to find a way to let him play in goal in the FA Cup Semi-Final — instead of Gary Plumley. And I myself was desperate to do something about Nigel Callaghan's hairstyle.'

'But something must be done. Since the summer, my great-grandson hasn't moved any further afield than Birmingham, but he's still getting more distant from the club with every passing day.'

Henry shook his head sadly. 'I really don't know what to advise,' he said. 'We can't expect Graham Taylor to come back again and make the club what it was — what it should be forever. We just have to hope someone else will do it for us.'

Now it was Florence's turn to gaze at the rag-rolled pastel wall-covering. In despair.

Henry gently patted the back of her hand and said: 'Keep the faith, young lady. Keep the faith.'

*   *   *

The day that everything changed was Tuesday 12th January.

Neville and Florence trudged reluctantly down Occupation Road and went through the ancient turnstile to Boothferry Park for Watford's FA Cup 3rd Round Replay against Second Division Hull City. All the signs were that Watford would be on the wrong end of a giant-killing. Very un-Graham Taylor.

But as soon as they arrived, there was a buzz in the Watford end among fans from the land of the living.

Neville and Florence immediately eavesdropped on a father and son.

'Halle-bloody-lujah!' the father said.

'What, Dad?' the boy asked.

'It's just been announced: Bassett's been sacked! Tom Walley's in charge tonight.'

'Halle-bloody-lujah!'

'Oi! Language, son!'

Neville turned to Florence in excitement.

'At last!' he said. 'We're getting our club back, Mother!'

Florence grabbed Neville. He grabbed her.

They jumped up and down.

They cheered.

They cried.

Watford could now be Watford again.

*   *   *

The following Saturday, January 16th, Watford had an away match at Wimbledon. Neville and Florence hurried down Occupation Road on their way to the ancient turnstile.

As soon as they arrived in the away end at Plough Lane, they heard the news. The club had a new manager. Steve Harrison. Watford's coach from the Taylor years. A Graham Taylor man.

Neville hugged his mother. Then, over her shoulder, he saw something he hadn't expected to see.

It was Tom and Mark.

Neville squealed with delight. He grabbed his mother's hand and took her over to stand with their descendants.

When the match kicked off, Neville noticed that his mother wasn't watching the game. She was watching

Tom and Mark. And she was wiping away tear after tear.

Neville wondered what had brought Tom and Mark to the game. Obviously they'd have heard that Bassett had been fired. But had that been enough? He listened out for clues, but heard nothing.

For the next 90 minutes, the game went well. With Bassett gone, and a Graham Taylor man at the helm, Watford actually won: 2-1. It was only three points, but the fans celebrated like they'd gained something far more significant.

After the final whistle, Neville heard Tom say to Mark: 'So. What do you think, lad? Worth the trip?'

Mark said eagerly: 'When's the next one?'

'Well, if we beat Hull in the second replay, the next round of the Cup is back at Coventry. Nice and local.'

'Brilliant. Count me in.'

'I will. As long as you join in me in the away end this time.'

Mark grinned and started rummaging in his coat pocket. The boy pulled out something small, slim, and blue — like a tiny hardback book without pages.

Neville and Florence stared at her 1920/21 season ticket. Tears flooded their eyes.

Mark waved the season ticket at his father and said

with a twinkle in his eye: 'With this thing you gave me, they'll let me in the Watford end for free, won't they?!'

Momentarily, Florence Simpson lost sight of her descendants. Her vision was too blurred. She couldn't see for happiness. Her fierce anger, and her previous extreme views about loyalty and family, were washed away.

Neville fought back the emotion of the moment. He was so proud of his son. Tom had done exactly what Neville had asked him to do on the terrace at Highfield Road back in October. Tom had given Mark the season ticket to show what Watford meant to him. Meant to all of the family.

He'd kept the Watford family together.

* * *

High in the main stand at Vicarage Road, at the next home game, Henry Grover said to Johnny Allgood: 'You know, Johnny, you were absolutely right about Bassett. He did have a huge and immediate impact at the club. And we'll definitely be remembering him for a very long time. Just not in a good way.'

'I'm not often wrong, Henry. And I'll tell you this

too. Watford Football Club is going to survive without Graham Taylor. What he built into the fabric of the club is so strong that it will last forever, whoever's in charge.'

'We're going to miss him awfully, though, aren't we?'

'Of course we are. This is just our first season after he's gone. There'll be many more, for the rest of eternity.'

'But how will we cope, Johnny?'

'Extremely well, Henry — as long as we concentrate on what he taught us. He's a fantastic human being, but he left us values that can outlive anyone on earth, sustaining this club forever. We just need to focus on those.'

'Golly, Johnny. You do know everything. So, er, one last question. An important one. Will we ever beat Luton again, at any point before the end of time? As of 1987, it really doesn't look like we will.'

Johnny chuckled.

'Everything is going to be fine, Henry. And at times it will be very fine indeed.'

THE END

2

DECONSTRUCTING HARRY

EARTH SEASON 2016/17

'Sir! Sir!' Derek Garston was saying. 'There's someone to see you, sir.'

'Hunh?' Bill Mainwood replied dopily. 'Tell them I'm…'

'It's urgent, sir! It's about Harry The Hornet! It can't wait!'

Bill Mainwood was in the programme office a couple of days after the 1-1 draw at home to Crystal Palace on Boxing Day 2016. He looked up and saw who Derek was talking about. She declared: 'Harry The Hornet should be sacked.'

Bill was surprised to see her in his office.

She continued: 'Harry shouldn't have ridiculed Wilfried Zaha by diving onto the grass. It's time to ditch our club mascot.'

Bill noticed a tremor in her voice. He wasn't sure whether it was anger or something else. Her face was giving nothing away. He said: 'Ditch Harry? But he was only having a bit of fun. That's his job.'

She stared at Bill and said: 'The club has to get rid of him.'

Bill thought this was an over-serious reaction. He looked deep into her unblinking eyes to try to gauge her feelings.

Then her voice cracked with emotion as she said: '…Just like they got rid of me in the early 2000s.'

Bill watched Harriet The Hornet's huge yellow head droop in sadness.

He took her black furry hand and patted it sympathetically.

* * *

Before today, Bill Mainwood hadn't seen Harriet Hornet for fifteen years or so. He took a good look at her now, here in Hornet Heaven. On the surface, she seemed a happy-go-lucky character, but Bill could tell her smile was just stitched-on. It was clear from her body language that she'd spent too long somewhere she didn't want to be. In this respect, it struck him, the six-foot polyester insect was a dead ringer for Jose Holebas.

'There, there,' Bill said.

Harriet began to sob. The black antennae on her yellow head wobbled.

Bill gently asked her why she was so unhappy. She explained that she was longing to be reunited with her husband.

'Every day I go back through the ancient turnstile to watch our wedding — on the pitch at home to Wolves on August 28th 1998,' she said. 'It's the only match in Hornet Heaven I ever re-visit.'

Bill felt a pang of pity in his chest. Poor Harriet was clearly still grief-stricken at her separation from Harry. He said: 'I know you'd like him to be up here with you, Harriet, but that would require his passing away. And surely no-one wants Harry The Hornet dead. Apart from Big Fat Sam, of course.'

Harriet seemed to recognise the truth of this. She covered her massive white eyes with her shaggy black hands and continued to weep.

Bill sat and thought. Hornet Heaven was a place where everyone was meant to be happy. So he began to wonder how he could cheer Harriet up, even if only temporarily.

Before long he had an idea.

*   *   *

In the atrium, a twenty-something lad was wearing Ray-Bans indoors.

'Boom! Man got one, innit, fam.'

The lad's friend, with a hipster beard, replied: 'What you got, dude?'

'Man got Watford players who are, like, cars, you get me.'

'Whoa! Totally wicked, dude!'

Bill explained to Harriet that Ray-Bans and Hipster loved making humorous lists involving Watford players. He hoped the lads would brighten her mood.

Harriet stared at them blankly with her big glued-on eyes.

Bill said: 'Ray-Bans, perhaps you should start — to let Harriet get the hang of things.'

'Sick! Man go first… Renault Gilmartin!'

'Nice one, dude,' Hipster said. 'How about… Walter Maserati.'

There wasn't a flicker on Harriet's face.

The lads kept going.

Ray-Bans said: 'Glenn Skoda.'

Hipster said: 'Tamas Prius-kin.'

Bill thought he'd better try and think of one — to jolly things along. He said: 'Vauxhall Vydra?' But then he wasn't sure whether that was actually a car or not.

Harriet started crying again.

* * *

Bill took Harriet to the club's swanky new restaurant — The Gallery — for a heart-to-heart.

At the door, they were stopped by Lamper — Hornet Heaven's former-hooligan-turned-chief-steward. 'Oi!' he said. 'You can't come in here wearing football kit!'

Harriet, in her old yellow shirt with the red sleeves, stepped forward. She was right in Lamper's face.

'Nice!' Lamper said. 'Want to make something of it, do ya? I like it tasty!'

Harriet shoved Lamper in the chest.

'Now we're talking!' Lamper said.

Lamper started windmilling. He landed his right fist in the middle of Harriet's furry face.

He waited for her to hit the deck. But Harriet didn't even flinch. She turned up her palms and beckoned Lamper on for more.

But Bill had seen enough. He got between them, calmed them down, and saw Harriet to a seat in one of the semi-circular booths.

Bill sat opposite and looked closely at Harriet Hornet. She was almost identical to Harry The Hornet. The only difference was that she had five vertical eyelashes stitched above each eye. They didn't make her look particularly feminine, Bill thought. Just permanently surprised. But he didn't say anything.

When the moment was right he said: 'Look, Harriet. I understand how you feel about Harry. We all get emotionally attached to people at the club. Too attached, sometimes. I mean, even our illustrious founder isn't immune.'

Bill pointed at Henry Grover — the man who founded Watford Rovers in 1881. Henry was sitting in a nearby booth, tearfully studying an old programme feature on Almen Abdi. The Father Of The Club lifted the programme to his lips and tenderly kissed Abdi on the cheek. The old man sniffled: 'I still love you, Almen.'

Bill said to Harriet: 'You see, it's important we all find a way to let go and move on.'

'But… I don't think I can,' Harriet said — and started sobbing again.

'You poor thing,' Bill said. 'Why don't you take off your head for a few moments and wipe your eyes?'

Harriet immediately stopped sobbing.

'Take my head off? What are you talking about?'

'Well, I know mascot rules dictate that you can't be seen out of costume, but surely you can't be expected to stay inside that ridiculous suit for the whole of eternity.'

There was a muffled sound as Harriet's furry hand slapped Bill on the cheek.

Bill was astonished. His eyes widened behind his spectacles.

Harriet slapped him again. Bill's spectacles went skewiff.

'Ridiculous suit?' she said.

'Sorry, I didn't mean to be rude. But you have to admit—'

'It's not a suit! This is my body! This is me!'

Bill frowned.

'You mean… You mean you're not a human being? You're not actually flesh and bone under there?'

Harriet's anger seeped away. She bowed her head again and said: 'I'm nothing but man-made fibre. I'm the only one of my type up here in Hornet Heaven. Which is why Harry The Hornet is the only person in the world for me. He's the only person the same as me.'

Bill was bit flummoxed by this. He re-adjusted his spectacles. Things were proving slightly odder than he'd expected.

He heard Derek's voice again: 'Sir! Sir! Excuse me, sir.'

Bill waved Derek away. This was the wrong moment to be interrupted. He needed to work out how there could be a non-human in Hornet Heaven. The idea was messing with his head. It seemed far too flaky to be real.

Harriet said: 'So. Aside from decapitating myself, have you got any other bright ideas how to help?'

Bill thought. He didn't have any actual ideas just yet, but he knew exactly what he needed to make happen.

Somehow — gently and delicately — he had to help

Harriet arrive at the realisation that, in the real world, Harry The Hornet was really just a bloke called Gareth.

* * *

Back in the atrium, Bill was ready with his idea. He said to Harriet: 'Right. Come along with me.'

'Where are we going?'

'On one of my Magical History Tours. I'm taking you to see games you've never seen before. Games from before you ever arrived at Watford,' he told her.

What he didn't tell her was that it was part of a masterplan to mend her broken heart by showing her the truth about Harry The Hornet.

* * *

Bill took Harriet down Occupation Road and through the ancient turnstile to a home game in 1980. On the Vicarage Road pitch, before the game, a costumed figure was presenting a giant cheque to a lady in a fur coat and glasses. Harriet started at the costume and said: 'What the hell is that?'

The costumed figure had a big letter W on its chest.

It had solid wings that somehow looked like shoulder pads from the TV drama Dynasty. It had jaunty yellow boots that seemed to be cast-offs from a psychedelic pantomime. And its head was clearly a yellow motorcycle helmet with antennae stuck on.

Harriet asked: 'Is it a walking jumble sale?'

Bill explained: 'That's actually Harry The Hornet. The first incarnation.'

Harriet said: 'Is someone taking the piss out of mascots?'

* * *

Next, they went to a game from a couple of years later into the 1980s.

Harriet watched, appalled, as two people paraded around the pitch in yellow and black costumes. They were wearing what looked like re-purposed fireside rugs — with floppy masks made from cut-offs of the same material. The costumes looked like they'd been made up from a design entered into a Junior Hornets design-a-mascot competition, under-fives section. And not the winning entry.

Harriet said: 'Is that seriously meant to be me and

Harry?'

She ran to the front of the terrace and shouted: 'Imposters!'

* * *

The next home game they went to was in the mid-1990s — when Harry The Hornet's costume actually looked a bit more like a hornet. Harriet admired the more realistically shaped yellow-and-red-striped abdomen. She was impressed by the huge white wings — which stuck out like sails on the creature's back. She said: 'Well, that's a bit better.'

But then she watched Harry The Hornet take part in a penalty shoot-out.

With Mr Blobby.

She clutched her brow and said: 'Oh God, this is just embarrassing.'

* * *

Later, at a match in 1996, they saw another different Harry The Hornet.

Harriet complained: 'So that's my future husband,

is it? What a prat. He's wearing his baseball cap sideways. And look at his arse. It's all saggy.'

Bill leaned in and said cheekily: 'Don't fancy yours much.'

When Harriet laughed, Bill realised his masterplan was already working.

*   *   *

Finally Bill took Harriet to the home game against Wolves in August 1998. Harry's costume was now the same as in 2016, apart from the shirt.

Bill said respectfully: 'So this was it. Your big day.'

They sat and watched the real-world version of Harriet getting married to Harry as part of the pre-match entertainment. Bill couldn't help wincing. Children in replica kit, clutching yellow and red balloons, formed a guard of honour as the two mascots walked hand in hand before the Sky Sports cameras. Harry's best man was the Wolverhampton mascot — Wolfie. Bill couldn't work out if it was meant to be a moving occasion, or what. A few people in the crowd looked up from their programmes, but they soon looked back down again.

Bill soon began to find it absolutely excruciating.

But he knew that, over the last fifteen years or so, Harriet had come back to witness this scene thousands of times.

He turned to see how she was coping this time around — now that she had a wider perspective on Watford's mascot history.

She took a deep breath and said: 'Go on, then. Tell me who's inside the ridiculous suits.'

Bill answered gently: 'It's actually just a couple of people from the club shop.'

Harriet stared at Bill as she processed this fact. She appeared wide-eyed, as always, but Bill could tell it wasn't shock. He knew she was coming to terms with the truth about mascots because she said: 'Jesus. It's all a bit shit, really, isn't it?'

* * *

Bill and Harriet Hornet returned to the present day. A couple of days later, on New Year's Day 2017, they went to the Spurs home game together.

They watched the current Harry The Hornet follow the Watford team out. The mascot lined up next to the Premier League arch and formally shook hands with the

Spurs players.

Bill had always been amazed that this regularly happened at Vicarage Road. He found it extraordinary. Before each match, the visiting team of high-profile elite athletes were obliged to shake hands with someone in an over-sized insect costume.

To Bill's mind this was just as disrespectful as Harry's dive behind Wilfried Zaha's back — the incident that had caused so much fuss after the Palace game. Yet no-one ever complained or even batted an eyelid: everyone took it seriously. Every season, they even let the cartoon insect take part in minute-silences to pay respects to the dead. It was bizarre. As bizarre as a non-human inhabiting Hornet Heaven, Bill thought to himself.

Now his musings were interrupted by Derek's voice again: 'Sir! Sir! This is important, sir!'

Bill waved Derek away again. He needed to make sure his masterplan with Harriet had reached its conclusion.

He glanced at her to see how she was coping with seeing the latest version of Harry The Hornet again.

Harriet noticed Bill looking at her and said: 'It's alright, thanks, Bill. I'm OK.'

Bill smiled.

She said: 'I'm cured. I'm not taking any of this seriously any more.'

'Good. I'm pleased. Very pleased,' Bill replied.

He cheerily patted her hairy hand and added: 'I wish I could say the same for everyone. And I include former England managers in that.'

* * *

'Sir! Sir! Are you alright, sir?'

'Hunh?'

'Sir!'

Bill fumbled dopily for his spectacles and lifted his head from the office desk.

'Gosh, you seem very drowsy, sir,' Derek said. 'I know the football hasn't been terribly entertaining recently, but honestly, sir, there's work to do and, as I say, there's someone to see you.'

Bill sat up straight. He cleared his throat and willed himself properly awake.

'Right,' he said. 'Now, who is it who wants to see me, young man?'

'A new arrival, sir. With news about Harry The

Hornet. Apparently, down on earth, there was talk of our mascot facing an FA charge for his dive after the Palace game.'

'What? A mascot in front of a disciplinary committee?'

'Yes, sir.'

'Seriously?'

'Yes, sir.'

Bill took off his spectacles and laid his head on the desk to doze again.

Sometimes, he thought to himself, the real world of football was stranger than fiction.

THE END

3

UP FOR THE CUP

EARTH SEASON 2016/17

'I hope you don't mind. I'd like a quiet word.'

It was the first week of January 2017. Henry Grover
— the man who'd founded Watford Rovers in 1881 —
was sitting on one of the yellow leather sofas in the
atrium. He'd perched himself next to one of Hornet
Heaven's relatively recent arrivals. The twenty-
something lad was wearing Ray-Ban Clubmasters
indoors.

Ray-Bans turned to Henry aggressively and said:
'Back off, fam, innit! Man done nuffin' wrong!'

Henry raised his hands in peace. He said: 'Golly,
I'm not suggesting that, Ray-Bans. Well, not yet,

anyway. It's just that a little bird told me you won't be bothering to go to the FA Cup tie against Burton Albion on Saturday.'

Ray-Bans relaxed. This was something he simply didn't care about. 'Nah, blud,' he said. 'Man not going.'

'But why not? It's the FA Cup — the most important competition in world football.'

'Ha! You is so out of date, fam!'

'I say, I don't believe I am.'

'Da FA Cup is tinpot, you get me, blud?'

Henry spluttered with indignation. 'The trophy is made of sterling 925 silver, I'll have you know.'

Henry narrowed his eyes and stared at Ray-Bans. This dismissive attitude to the FA Cup was exactly where modern football was going wrong, he told himself.

He stood up. He would change Ray-Bans's mind. Before Saturday.

* * *

'I agree with you, Henry.'

Henry had popped into the office of Bill Mainwood, Hornet Heaven's Head of Programmes. He was in search of ideas for persuading Ray-Bans that the FA Cup was still a worthwhile competition.

Bill continued: 'It breaks my heart that young people don't appreciate the heritage of the FA Cup.'

'That's not fair, sir! I definitely appreciate it, sir!'

Derek Garston — Bill's 13-year-old assistant — had an encyclopaedic knowledge of Watford stats. And he loved to show it off.

'Since 1886, sir,' the boy said, 'we've played 345 FA Cup matches. We've won 158 and lost 119, sir.'

Henry found Derek's smugness irritating. He didn't like complacency. It was exactly what had led the FA into undermining its once-respected cup competition.

'Ah, but I'm afraid you're missing the point, Derek. Watford's cup heritage isn't about numbers, you see. It's about glory.'

'Glory, Mr Grover, sir? Are you referring to the fact that, over the years, we've defeated every single one of what the modern fan knows as the Big Five: Liverpool in 1970, Manchester United in 1982, Manchester City in 1986, Chelsea in 1987, and Arsenal in 1987 and 2016.'

'Ah. That's much better, young chap,' Henry said. 'A modern fan like Ray-Bans will definitely be able to relate to that. Beating Arsenal last season proved that, even in the present day, the FA Cup can still bring enormous joy to Watford fans. Well done, young fellow. Those stats are wonderfully uplifting.'

Derek replied: 'Except, of course, that the competition has now been devalued by most top flight teams putting out weakened sides in the early rounds, Mr Grover, sir.'

Henry wasn't so keen on this fact.

'Also by the winners being given a place in the Europa League,' the boy added. 'The Europa League! It's ridiculous, Mr Grover, sir! Win the final, these days, and they hand you a booby prize!'

Henry really didn't want to hear this. He put his fingers in his ears and left the office.

* * *

Henry needed somewhere to think. He walked down Occupation Road and went through the ancient turnstile that allowed residents of Hornet Heaven to re-visit any Watford game from the past. He went back to October 23rd 1886 and stood on the touchline at Rose & Crown Meadow — the home ground of Watford Rovers at the time. The game in front of him was the club's first ever

FA Cup tie — against Swindon Town.

As he watched, he began to wonder if he'd got things all wrong. Maybe it was his own perspective that was out of kilter — not the modern world's. Maybe he'd always attached too much importance to the FA Cup because this particular game, here before his eyes, was the club's very first competitive game in its history. And maybe — also — because he himself had played in it.

He watched the 20-year-old version of himself — in defence — win a tackle and lump the ball upfield. He winced. It lacked finesse. Troy Deeney would definitely have given him a mouthful for the quality of service to the forwards.

Henry sighed and trooped back to the ancient turnstile. He probably needed to accept reality: the FA Cup had had its day, and he'd never convince Ray-Bans otherwise.

* * *

Henry trudged into the atrium, head bowed. He went over to one of the yellow sofas, ready to slump down into it.

Suddenly he felt a gentle hand on his arm. A voice

said: 'No you don't, Henry.'

Henry turned and saw the kind smiling face of Bill Mainwood.

Bill continued: 'After your conversation with Derek I realised I couldn't stand idly by. So I've organised a little something to try and put things right. You're coming with us.'

Henry peered beyond Bill and saw a huge crowd of Hornet Heaven residents. Derek was at the front, with dozens of former Watford players behind him. Henry spotted genuine legends such as Johnny Allgood, Cliff Holton, Tommy Barnett, and Arthur Woodward. He saw several recent arrivals in the crowd too — fans who had more modern attitudes to football: Frank Gammon, Pete Pickles and Ray-Bans's mate Hipster. Ray-Bans himself was loitering to one side. He didn't look like he wanted to be there.

Bill said: 'We're all going on one of my Magical History Tours. An FA Cup Special. Revisiting classic matches.'

Henry thought that revisiting epic Cup games was a brilliant idea. He felt a surge of excitement. He called out to Ray-Bans jubilantly: 'Boom! What is you waitin' for, blud? Mandem is up for da Cup!'

* * *

The group went, en masse, to some of the best occasions in Watford's entire history.

Hipster said the 4-3 win over Luton in the third round in 1984 was totally amazing. Dude.

Ray-Bans said the 1984 semi-final victory over Plymouth was sick. And dench.

After that, Pete Pickles had the idea of watching the quarter-final wins over Arsenal — in 1987 and 2016 — back to back. It was totally brilliant. Everyone had the time of their afterlives.

In fact, there were so many incredible games to watch that the Magical History Tour was into its third day when, back on Occupation Road, Bill announced it was time to stop. It was now Saturday 7th January.

Ray-Bans protested: 'But man is lovin' dis, blud. No way is man stoppin', fam, you get me.'

Bill gave Ray-Bans a kindly smile and said: 'But you don't have to stop. The 2017 third round starts today for Watford — against Burton. We could have another amazing cup run. Watford are just six wins from glory. Historic, eternal glory.'

Henry was listening to Bill's words. They soothed his heart.

But the words did more than that for Ray-Bans. The words had him running back to the atrium, desperate to grab a programme for the match against Burton.

'Historic, fam! Eternal, blud! Glory, innit!'

*   *   *

Back in the atrium, Henry went up to Bill. He wasn't convinced Ray-Bans's new enthusiasm would survive Watford's terrible current form. But he was grateful for Bill's intervention. He said: 'Thank you, my old friend. The FA Cup has regained its magic. For now, at least.'

Bill said: 'We need to be realistic. The Burton game is bound to disappoint. Then the draw will probably give us a potential banana skin in the next round. I wouldn't be surprised if I need to do another Magical History Tour later in the competition — to re-enthuse people. That's why I kept something up my sleeve.'

'Really?' Henry said, intrigued. 'What have you got up there, Bill? What's up your sleeve?'

'Wembley, 1984. Today's young Watford fans weren't there. So they can't quite imagine what it would feel like to watch a single game that could write the club's name on the game's greatest trophy forever.'

Henry felt his eyes misting — less at the memory, more at the prospect of it happening again.

'Good lord, Bill. Just… Good lord.'

Bill saw Henry's eyes. He knew what was coming. He hurriedly took off his glasses — to ensure he'd go through eternity still able to see.

Sure enough, Henry threw his arms wide and wrapped Bill in a bear-hug as warm and solid as the tradition of the FA Cup itself.

THE END

4

NOT QUITE MANAGING

EARTH SEASONS 2012-2015

'What a beautiful afternoon!' Neil McBain declared, unusually contentedly.

'I'm not sure anything at Selhurst Park could ever be described as beautiful,' Mike Keen replied in his normal world-weary way.

On the opening day of the 2012/13 season, two former Watford managers were in the away section at a sunlit Selhurst Park just before the teams came out. Neil McBain was a hard-drinking and hard-gambling Scot who'd managed Watford in the 1930s and 1950s. Mike Keen, sitting next to McBain, had been boss between 1973 and 1977.

'Ach, cheer up!' McBain said. 'It's the first day of the new season. A time for optimism. Sean Dyche did a great job last year. The Ginger Ninja. The Throaty Goatee. I can't wait to see how he gets on in his second season of management with us.'

'Well, you'll be waiting a long time,' Mike replied. 'Dychey's been given the old heave-ho.'

'What? Why? He was doing a grand job. Who's in charge now, then?'

'The new owners have installed Gianfranco Zola as Head Coach.'

'Why are you telling me that? Who cares about the coach? Tell me who the manager is.'

'There isn't going to be a manager.'

'What? But that's not possible. How can a team not have a manager?'

'The Head Coach is the Gaffer.'

'No! This is wrong!'

'It's the new-fangled way.'

'It's definitely wrong! Completely wrong! Mark my words: no good can possibly come of this for Watford Football Club!'

McBain stood and steamed. He said: 'This is a change too far! You can't get rid of managers!'

'Well, that's not entirely true, is it,' Mike replied. 'The club got rid of me. They got rid of you twice.'

McBain smarted at the reminder. He looked round. He saw another former manager was joining them. It was Harry Kent — the man who'd become Watford's second-ever boss in 1910.

'Kent!' McBain said. 'Have you heard what's happened?'

'Yes,' Kent replied in his sparse, clipped way. 'It's precipitate.' Harry Kent was a strait-laced man of few words, and sometimes quite old-fashioned ones. 'Peremptory,' he added.

McBain said: 'Good. At last something we can agree on, Kent.'

McBain and Kent had never really got on in Hornet Heaven. Kent had heard the stories from the 1950s about McBain regularly stopping the team coach at a pub in Rickmansworth so he could get a drink. Harry Kent didn't approve.

McBain continued: 'The manager's job at Watford has always been about much more than just coaching.'

'Yes. I recall your role encompassed drinking and gambling,' Kent said.

'Ha ha. Mock me if you like, but I contributed over

and above. In 1932, I dug a new staircase into the banking at the Vicarage Road end.'

'The sole enduring feature of your tenure…'

'Watch it, Kent!'

'…before you sought employment at the club that dare not speak its name.'

'For God's sake, how many times do I have to tell you, Kent! Shut up about that!'

Mike Keen tried to make peace between the managers. 'Come on,' he said, 'let's not argue. In our time, all of us were important to the club.'

McBain and Kent found themselves able to agree on this.

But Keen couldn't help adding: 'Until we weren't important any more.'

For a few moments, the three ex-managers sat silently, contemplating this truth. The scars from their departures still ran deep.

McBain said: 'My point remains. We weren't just "coaches". We were the managers. And football teams need managers.'

Suddenly there was a roar as the Palace and Watford teams emerged onto the pitch. The three men watched.

Harry Kent said: 'Observe, gentlemen. We are going to have a manager after all. A multitude, in fact.'

Neil McBain and Mike Keen wondered what Kent was talking about. Then they noticed that every single Watford player had the words 'Football Manager' on the front of their shirts.

Kent said: 'Must be their new job titles.'

'Eleven managers?' Mike said. 'That's extremely new-fangled.'

'This is a nonsense!' McBain spluttered. 'They can't all be the manager! Especially if one of them's Joe Garner!'

McBain turned away in disgust. He noticed a real-world fan who was sitting a few seats along. The fan also had the words Football Manager on her brand new shirt.

'Her as well?' he said in disbelief. 'But she's a fan! What does she know?'

He swore. He looked deeper into the stand. He swore again and said: 'Look! There's hundreds of them that have been appointed manager!'

Harry Kent coughed. He said: 'I was jesting about it being a job title, McBain.'

'You, Kent? Joking?'

'Football Manager is the name of the new sponsor.'

'Right. I see. So strait-laced Harry Kent does comedy these days, does he?'

Harry Kent ran a finger beneath his wing collar to loosen it. He said: 'I'm changing with the times. I do epic banter now.'

'Well, change isn't always for the better,' McBain said. 'Believe me: Watford will never get promoted to the Premier League as long as they have a Head Coach instead of a manager.'

Mike Keen said: 'Oh God. Really? Never is a long time in Hornet Heaven.'

'I know what I'm talking about,' McBain insisted. 'If I'm wrong, I'll… I'll eat my hat.'

Harry Kent's strict morals — and his disregard for Neil McBain's morals — meant he never let the Scotsman get away with anything. He said: 'You don't have a hat.'

'Alright, I'll eat someone else's, then. You watch me. I'll eat the biggest hat in Hornet Heaven!'

Harry Kent was a man who rarely smiled, but he did so now.

He said: 'I shall hold you to that, McBain.'

* * *

'Who's Baldy?' McBain asked.

A short hairless man was frantically waving his arms in Watford's technical area. It was fourteen months later: December 21st 2013. McBain was sitting in the away stand at Portman Road with Mike Keen.

'"Baldy" is called "Beppe", it says here,' Mike replied, looking up from the Ipswich programme. 'They've got rid of Zola. Shame. He was a nice man.'

'Nice counts for nothing,' McBain said. 'Zola was never going to get us promoted. Besides, he was only Head Coach. You need a manager.'

'He got us pretty close,' Mike said.

Neil McBain cast his mind back to the end of the previous season — when Watford so nearly won automatic promotion to the Premier League. As he did so, he noticed that Skilly Williams was squeezed into the seat in front of him. Skilly was arguably the best goalkeeper in the first 75 years of Watford history, and certainly the podgiest. On the field, the man used to wear his shorts almost up to his nipples and, here in Hornet Heaven, he still wore the huge, round, flat cap he'd regularly sported between 1913 and 1926. It was the biggest hat in Hornet Heaven.

McBain looked at Skilly's hat. He swallowed hard. If Watford had beaten either Leeds or Crystal Palace back in May, it would have been knife and fork time.

McBain focused on the new man in the technical area again. He asked Mike Keen: 'So is Beppe's job title Head Coach or Manager?'

'Head Coach.'

Neil McBain shook his head. Watford would never win promotion. He said: 'We're doomed.'

* * *

Eight months later, away to Charlton, in September 2014, Neil McBain sat with Mike Keen in the Jimmy Seed stand at The Valley. McBain stared at the dark-haired man in Watford's technical area.

'Who's Beardy?' McBain asked.

Mike Keen knew where this was going. 'Oscar Garcia,' he replied. 'And, yes, he's Head Coach, not manager.

Neil McBain glanced at Skilly Williams' massive hat a few rows away. He said: 'No need for ketchup any time soon.'

* * *

Four games later, McBain and Keen sat in the Rookery End for the home match with Brentford. McBain gazed glumly at another new man in the technical area.

'Who's…?'

He sighed. The new man was clean-shaven with a full head of hair.

McBain said: 'I don't know how to describe him. The club's got through so many head coaches, they've run out of people with distinguishing features.'

* * *

Two games later, at Sheffield Wednesday, yet another new man was prowling the technical area at Hillsborough. Neil McBain clutched his head as he sat next to Mike Keen.

'You think they'd learn their lesson and get a manager, not a Head Coach,' he moaned. 'Oscar Garcia lasted four games. Billy McKinlay lasted two. At the current rate, this will be Slavisa Jokanovic's only match.'

Mike replied: 'If the current rate continues, the next one will leave at half-time on Tuesday night against Forest.'

Mike Keen thought some more about the maths of the situation. He quickly worked out that, if each new Head Coach continued lasting half as long as the previous one, the planet would run out of available human beings before the final whistle blew against Forest.

'Why can't they just appoint a proper manager?' McBain whined. 'I really want us to get promoted to the Premier League.'

McBain glanced at Skilly Williams who was sitting nearby in the row in front. McBain said: 'You know, things are getting so desperate I reckon I might actually be glad to…'

'Glad to… what?' Mike asked.

'What I'm saying is: promotion feels so far away that I'd... I'd just like a taste of it.'

'What are you talking about?'

McBain gazed at Skilly Williams's hat. He ran his tongue around his lips. He said: 'Pass me Skilly's hat, would you? I just want a little lick.'

* * *

Eight matches later, Slavisa Jokanovic was still in charge for the away game against Fulham at Craven Cottage on December 5th 2014 — though Neil McBain wasn't quite sure how. Watford had lost their last four games. McBain was itching for the doomed Head Coach experiment to end.

Despite this, he and Mike Keen thoroughly enjoyed the early part of the match — especially when Fulham's goalkeeper was sent off for giving away the penalty that put Watford 2-0 up after twenty minutes. In front of them, Skilly Williams manoeuvred his sizeable frame so he could stand on his seat. Skilly started a chant: 'Dodgy keeper! Dodgy keeper!'

McBain laughed. He pointed at Skilly and chanted: 'Podgy keeper! Podgy keeper!'

All the Hornet Heaven residents in the Putney End joined in. Mike Keen didn't stop giggling until Troy Deeney scored Watford's third another 17 minutes later.

At half-time, McBain bumped into Harry Kent.

'Haven't seen you for a while,' McBain said.

'I've been busy,' Kent replied. 'Occupying myself with something you should have done, McBain.

Studying how to be a better manager.'

'Well, you won't get better by watching Head Coaches — especially this Joka joker. He's lucky Fulham are so terrible. There's no way we're getting promoted.'

'I haven't been observing Head Coaches. I've been learning from a computer.'

'What? Where did you develop computer skills? You died in 1948.'

'It's called "Football Manager". You must remember the sponsor on the team shirt?'

'Of course I do. But what is "Football Manager"?'

'It's a simulation.'

'Isn't that what Fernando Forestieri gets booked for?'

Harry Kent sighed. He took McBain to stand over the shoulder of a fan from the land of the living who was playing Football Manager on an iPhone. Kent explained all the statistical variables that, within the computer game, could be altered to affect the outcome of matches.

McBain said: 'Ach, this is completely unrealistic. Where's the button that lets you shout at players more? In our day as managers, that was all we needed. Shouting. And a few extra knees-bends. Those were the key to success.'

Kent pointed out examples of the tactical choices available within the simulation game.

McBain started to grumble. 'This kind of stuff never existed in our day,' he said. 'It's not fair.'

'Why?' Kent asked.

'It gives modern day Head Coaches the chance to be better than we were as managers.'

'Not just Head Coaches,' Kent said. 'It means that even fans know far more than we did.'

Kent corrected himself. 'Well, they *think* they know more.'

'No change there, then,' McBain said.

McBain carried on watching the fan playing Football Manager. He asked Kent: 'So who collects all the data and turns it into a game? That person must know more about football than anyone else on the planet.'

'He's called Miles Jacobson,' Kent replied. 'He's a Watford fan. Come with me. He's here tonight.'

* * *

As the second half kicked off, Kent and McBain found

Miles Jacobson sitting in the Directors' Box next to Gino Pozzo.

McBain stared at Jacobson. He said: 'This guy? How can this guy know more about football than anyone else on the planet? Look at the state of him!'

'Hold your tongue and listen,' Kent said. 'You'll learn something.'

Miles Jacobson said to Gino Pozzo: 'Three nil up, away from home, you need to switch to a counter-attacking set-up. We should sit deep and bring on fast-breaking midfielders. Lloyd Dyer's on the bench. He's just the man for this situation.'

Neil McBain couldn't stop himself from laughing. 'Lloyd Dyer?! Ha! I wouldn't have him in my under-nines team!'

'Miles will be proved correct,' Harry Kent insisted. 'Wait and see.'

Jacobson continued: 'Almen Abdi's done brilliantly tonight, but he's not the fastest. Slav needs to take Abdi off and bring on Dyer.'

Harry Kent nodded. He said: 'Profoundly wise words. Miles Jacobson is truly omniscient.'

Kent and McBain turned back to the pitch. Twenty five yards out, Almen Abdi received the ball, took one touch, and fired it into the top corner of Fulham's goal.

Neil McBain screamed with joy. He grabbed Harry Kent round the head and jumped up and down. He laughed and laughed.

'Ha! That's what I bloody love about football!' he said. 'No-one actually knows bloody anything!'

* * *

From that day on, Neil McBain, Harry Kent and Mike Keen spent hours and hours watching fans play Football Manager. Like thousands of people all over the world, they became addicted to it.

They also began to feel knowledgeable about football in a way that hadn't been available to them when they were the managers. It turned out that shouting and knees-bends probably hadn't been the key to success after all — though Neil McBain still believed that, even today, the cure for all on-field injuries was cold water. The 'magic sponge', he thought, should definitely be built into the Football Manager game engine.

On the 24th January 2015, the three of them went to the home game against Blackpool. Watford were in sixth place in the league table and Jokanovic was still in charge. But the Horns reached half-time two nil down. The situation looked irretrievable.

McBain said: 'Back in my day, I wouldn't have had a clue how to turn this around.'

Kent replied: 'Must have been the whisky.'

'That's a cheap shot, Kent.'

'Just like your whisky, McBain.'

'Shut up,' McBain said. 'What I mean is: here in 2015, thanks to Football Manager, I know exactly what needs to change.'

Mike Keen said: 'Go on, then. What's the answer?'

'It's obvious,' McBain explained. 'In a situation like this, a team needs a bits-and-pieces goalscorer — someone who's always in the right place at the right time. But Odion Ighalo's Football Manager rating for his positioning skills is only eight. That's below par. We definitely need to sub him off. Definitely.'

But when Watford took the field for the second half, the player that Slavisa Jokanovic had subbed off at half-time was Tommie Hoban. Ben Watson came on.

Neil McBain said: 'Big mistake.'

Watford promptly scored seven goals in the second half. The sixth goal came when Troy Deeney's shot cannoned back from a post and smacked off the head of the perfectly positioned Odion Ighalo. Ighalo had his hat-trick.

McBain burst out laughing. He danced with joy. He grappled with Mike Keen and Harry Kent in a tangle of leaping limbs.

'Ha!' he shouted. 'Again! No-one knows bloody anything! Especially me!'

But as he headed for the ancient turnstile afterwards, McBain thought about the Head Coach's pivotal half-time substitution. He began to think that Jokanovic did actually have what was required to get Watford promoted after all. Even though the man didn't have the job title of 'manager'.

McBain went out onto Occupation Road and saw a crowd of Edwardian Watford fans hurling their hats into the air in excitement at the most incredible second half turnaround they'd ever seen. McBain was excited too. So excited that, when he noticed Skilly Williams's hat flying higher than anyone else's, he was tempted to go and catch it between his teeth, and get chomping straightaway.

*   *   *

The penultimate game of the 2014/15 season was away at Brighton at the Amex Stadium. For months, Jokanovic had been successfully tweaking formations and tactics during games. Watford were now top of the table, but needed to win their final two matches to be certain of promotion to the Premier League.

Neil McBain, Mike Keen and Harry Kent went to the match together. But after 20 minutes, they were feeling frustrated. It was still 0-0. Watford were getting nowhere.

'Something has to change,' Mike said. 'What does Football Manager say we should do?'

'I witnessed a fan playing earlier,' Kent said. 'He had the answer.'

'Great. What was it?'

'He replaced Juan Carlos Paredes with Cristiano Ronaldo.'

The three of them carried on watching for another five minutes. Watford still weren't making any headway.

'It's going to be OK,' McBain said. 'Joka will see us right. In Joka I trust.'

'You've changed your tune,' Mike said. 'You do know he's still only Head Coach, not Manager? You said we'd never win promotion under a Head Coach.'

'I did say that. But I'm ready to admit that people like us have no idea how football actually works. Even after studying Football Manager.'

'But we were real managers.'

'Aye. And we didn't have a clue. If we'd known how football actually works, we'd all have won every week.'

'So what about Joka? Does he know how football works?'

'We're just about to find out.'

They looked across to the technical area. Jokanovic was making a tactical substitution after 26 minutes. Daniel Tozser was coming on for Ikechi Anya.

Mike Keen looked vacantly at Harry Kent and shrugged. Harry Kent looked vacantly at Neil McBain and shrugged. Neil McBain shrugged back.

'In Joka I trust,' McBain said.

Three minutes later, the ball dropped to Odion Ighalo in the Brighton penalty area at the far end. Ighalo flicked it to Troy Deeney. Deeney took a touch with his left and dispatched the ball with his right. Watford were 1-0 up. McBain, Keen and Kent grabbed each other and bounced ecstatically for a full two minutes, oblivious to anything except their own joy.

Eventually, Neil McBain broke away from the others. He hurdled the advertising hoardings and sprinted onto the pitch. Play had re-started, but McBain ran past Gabriele Angella and Matt Connolly. He arrived at the touchline by the technical area. He knelt down in front of Slavisa Jokanovic. He raised his arms and bowed down, over and over again, to Watford's greatest gaffer in a decade — regardless of job title.

* * *

Fifty minutes later, just before the hour mark of the Brighton match, Neil McBain made his way to the Directors' Box. He was so excited about Jokanovic's success in the dug-out that he wanted to eavesdrop on what Gino Pozzo might be saying about the brilliant Head Coach. He was convinced the owner must be planning to give Joka a juicy new contract in the Premier League.

As he entered the Directors' Box, McBain spotted Miles Jacobson again. Jacobson was saying: 'One nil up, away from home, you need to switch to a counter-attacking set-up.'

McBain was pretty sure he'd heard this before

somewhere.

'Vydra's on the bench,' Jacobson continued. 'He's just the man for this situation.'

'Oh, give it a rest, Jacobson!' McBain cried. 'What do your computers know? Joka's the man who knows!'

McBain sat down next to Gino and cocked an ear for any idle chatter about a new contract for the Head Coach.

Five minutes later, Matej Vydra came on for Odion Ighalo. Thirty-five minutes later, in added time, Craig Cathcart played the ball down the line to Troy Deeney to start a counter-attack. Deeney took the ball on and looked up. In the middle, unmarked, was Matej Vydra. Troy swung the ball across. Vydra chested it down, took a touch with his right and dispatched the ball with his left. The away end beyond him exploded with yellow noise.

Neil McBain leaped out of his seat. He raised his arms to the sky. Tears started to pour down his cheeks. He turned and saw Miles Jacobson jumping up and down, hugging anyone and everyone. McBain ran over and planted a huge kiss on Jacobson's face. Did Jacobson know anything about football? Did his computers? McBain didn't care. All that mattered was that these people were Watford and these people were very, very happy.

*　*　*

Two and three-quarter hours later, in the land of the living, Watford's promotion to the Premier League was confirmed when Middlesbrough and Norwich dropped points in their afternoon games. But this wonderful news had no way of reaching Hornet Heaven. So the residents had an anxious week, not knowing what Watford would need to do in the final game to win promotion.

The following Saturday, Neil McBain, Mike Keen and Harry Kent gathered in the atrium to await the arrival of the programme for the final match of the season at home to Sheffield Wednesday. It would tell them the results of the other matches since the final whistle at Brighton.

The atrium was packed. Neil McBain looked around. He was tingling with nerves. He reckoned every single Watford fan in Hornet Heaven must be there, waiting for the programme, feeling exactly the same way. There'd be people, he realised, who had supported the club under every manager from Johnny Allgood in

1903 to Slavisa Jokanovic in 2015. And, yes, he was calling Slavisa Jokanovic a manager, as far as he was concerned.

McBain turned to his friends to see how the nervous wait was affecting them. Mike Keen looked absolutely worn out. Nothing new there. Harry Kent was standing erect in his dark suit. He had his hands behind his back.

McBain said: 'You look tense, Kent. Are you ready for this?'

'I am fully prepared,' Kent replied. 'But I don't think you are.'

'Oh, I'm more ready than I've ever been,' McBain said. 'This season I've learned a lot about how football works. From Football Manager. From Joka. But also from the patch of sand in our penalty area at the Amex Stadium that made a definite Brighton equaliser bounce wide in a way no-one could possibly have predicted. So I'm ready for anything.'

'No, you're not.'

'I promise you I am.'

Harry Kent brought his hands out from behind his back. He was holding Skilly Williams's huge cloth cap.

McBain took the hat. He said: 'I see. OK. Well, I definitely am ready now. That looks… delicious.'

Suddenly, a cry went up: 'Programme's in!'

A hush came over the atrium. Now everyone in Hornet Heaven would hear what had happened since the Brighton game. Bill Mainwood, Head of Programmes, stepped forward and plucked a copy of the Sheffield Wednesday programme from the shelf. Without glancing at it, he took it over to Henry Grover, The Father Of The Club.

Henry composed himself. He peered down at the golden front cover. He read three words at the top of the page and looked up. Every eye in Hornet Heaven was trained on him. His own eyes started to fill. The three words had been 'Souvenir Promotion Edition'.

Henry threw the programme in the air and shouted: 'We're up!'

The whole of Hornet Heaven shrieked and roared and cheered and howled.

The glass of the atrium shook.

The floor reverberated.

People jumped.

People hugged.

People cried.

In the middle of it all, Neil McBain stood and watched, soberly taking the moment in, absorbing how much it meant to how many people.

Then he lifted Skilly's hat and, with a big smile, took a great big, happy bite.

THE END

5

FANZINES ARE BAD FOR YOU

EARTH SEASON 2015/16

'Not another fanzine!'

Bill Mainwood waved his arm dismissively. The gesture made him look exactly like Jose Holebas — except for the white hair, spectacles and complete absence of tattoos.

Bill was the man in charge of programmes in Hornet Heaven. He had no time for non-club publications. In fact, when it came to unofficial journalism about Watford, Bill pledged commitment to the same approach that Jose Holebas wore tattooed across his chest: 'Trust Nobody'.

'Remember, young man,' Bill said sternly to his 13-

year-old assistant as they stood at the programme shelves. 'People shouldn't always believe what they read.'

Derek Garston nodded at his boss's wise words. Then he squeaked: 'Apparently, the new fanzine's going to be called Hornet Effect, sir.'

'Well, it can Hornet Eff-off.'

'I beg your pardon, sir?'

'Fanzines are bad for you. Compared to the official programme, they're far too…'

'Too what, sir?'

Bill thought for a moment. He needed to find exactly the right word.

'Far too much fun, young man.'

'Fun? But that's a good thing, sir. The official programme is so boring.'

Bill scowled at his assistant. He didn't take kindly to this kind of talk. It undermined the integrity of the very thing to which he'd dedicated his afterlife. He replied: 'The official programme is a respectable publication, Derek. An upstanding organ.'

'But have you ever seen anyone actually read it, sir?'

Bill gasped at his assistant's insolence. He grabbed

Derek by the ear and said: 'As a matter of fact, I'm about to see someone read 50 of them! As punishment!'

Bill led Derek, by the ear, to the programme office. He locked the boy in.

*　*　*

Derek sat behind the desk and yawned as he turned the pages of the 43rd programme of his punishment. It was from the final game of the 1977/78 season, at home to Southport. It was dull, dull, dull.

But then, suddenly, it wasn't. On page 22 he saw a full-page advertisement for the Top Man menswear shop on the High Street. It featured a photograph of a pouting blonde lady. Wearing a leotard. Off both shoulders. Revealing an ample amount of bosom.

Derek felt a sensation he'd never experienced from reading a programme before.

The 13-year-old glanced up at the door to check that his boss wasn't looking. Then he sat and stared at the photograph for a very long time.

*　*　*

Derek was startled when the door burst open.

'Quick, Derek, I need you in the atrium. Right now!'

Derek hurriedly closed the Southport programme. He looked up at Bill from behind the desk. He didn't get up. He blushed.

'Come on!' Bill demanded. 'On your feet!'

'But, sir…'

Bill could tell something was going on. 'But what, young man?'

Derek's face reddened even more.

Bill went over to the desk. He grabbed the Southport programme. He flicked through and arrived at page 22.

'Derek! This is rude and dirty!'

'Don't blame me, sir!' Derek protested. 'It's the official programme. To quote your own words, sir, it's a respectable publication. You said it's an—'

Derek stopped. He decided not to use the words "upstanding organ".'

But Bill wasn't listening. He grabbed another pile of fifty programmes and locked Derek in again.

* * *

Derek stared at the pile of programmes and sulked. He gazed around the office.

In the corner was a cupboard. He'd never paid attention to it before. Now he noticed it was double-padlocked. He became curious. Why would Bill be keeping certain programmes under lock and key?

He grabbed a paper clip from the desk, bent it, and set about the padlocks.

Before long, he'd unlocked them. He looked back at the office door to check Bill wasn't there again.

Then he opened the cupboard.

* * *

Bill walked into the office and saw Derek with his feet up on the desk, laughing. The boy was reading a copy of Look At The Stars.

'Sir, these Robbo diaries are absolute genius!'

Bill looked at the desk. It was strewn with copies of Mud Sweat And Beers, The Yellow Experience, Clap Your Hands Stamp Your Feet, The Watford Book Of Soccer, All Watford All Lovin' It, The Horn, and Golden Pages.

Derek had found Bill's secret stash of Watford fanzines from down the years.

It was Bill's turn to blush. He closed the door to make sure no-one could overhear. Then he sat down. 'I love fanzines,' he said quietly.

'What? But, sir, you said—'

'I know what I said. I said it because… Well, programmes are an essential part of our afterlives in Hornet Heaven. We couldn't go to games without them. They need to be respected.'

Derek nodded. He could see where Bill was coming from.

'But fanzines add so much. Different voices. Different perspectives. Creativity. They get fans thinking in a way the official programme can never inspire.'

'Does that mean you're happy there's going to be a new one, sir — this Hornet Effect thing?'

Bill's face changed. Suddenly he looked as distrusting of fanzines as he'd looked earlier. 'We need to wait and see what's in it,' he said.

'Why, sir?'

'Because I heard a rumour that it's going to feature a story about you and me.'

Derek looked alarmed as he realised the story might

depict him doing something embarrassing. Fanzines really could be bad for you.

'But it's like I said before,' Bill reassured him with a smile. 'People shouldn't always believe what they read.'

THE END

6

BORING BORING WATFORD

EARTH SEASON 2016/17

On the first day of April 2017, Henry Grover and Neil McBain were at Watford's Premier League home game against Sunderland.

McBain, who'd managed the Hornets in the 1930s and 1950s, reckoned the team were playing the least exciting football he'd seen since Henry founded the club in 1881.

'Ach, this is like watching paint dry,' McBain moaned.

Henry took offence. He said crossly: 'Excuse me, McBain, but no it isn't.'

'Come off it, Henry. I know you're The Father Of

The Club and all that, but you've got to admit it. Watching our football at the moment is definitely like watching paint dry.'

'No, it isn't.'

'Ach, get a grip, man. You can't pretend that Walter Mazzarri's football isn't boring.'

'What? Oh. I see.'

Henry chuckled at his new-found understanding.

'Of course the football's boring!' he agreed. 'Completely boring! I was offended because comparing it to paint-drying gives paint-drying a bad name. And I'm not having that. I'd far rather be watching some gorgeous paint effects — stencilling, perhaps, or sponging — as they sacrifice their pristine wetness on a pastel eggshell base. Goodness, yes. That would be right royal entertainment compared to this heap of tripe!'

* * *

When the soul-destroying tedium of the 1-0 win over Sunderland was over, Neil McBain and Henry Grover returned through the ancient turnstile and walked up Occupation Road. In the past, Hornet Heaven had always been bathed in a sunshine that everyone had assumed was eternal. But in recent weeks, the light had been flat and grey — as if a cloud was hanging over the place.

McBain said to Henry: 'Ach, our football is as colourless as this weather. How can I be fanatical about a team that keeps passing the ball backwards and sideways? I call it Walter's Waltz. Back-side-side, back-side-side. It's slow and it's dull — even when we win. It's got to the point where I don't even want to talk about Watford. Or think about Watford.'

Henry took a deep breath, ready to give a pep-talk befitting The Father Of The Club. He felt a duty to inspire McBain with the need for eternal commitment as a Watford fan — even when there's little to enjoy on the pitch.

But then he breathed out — as his own boredom at Mazzarri's football overcame him.

'Oh God! I think I'm losing the will to live. In an eternal paradise!'

* * *

Three days later, at the top of Occupation Road, Henry bumped into Bill Mainwood, Hornet Heaven's Head Of

Programmes. In the lacklustre light, Bill said: 'Hello, Henry. Been to a game?'

Henry hid the programme he was carrying. 'Maybe. Maybe not,' he replied. 'But less about me, old chap. How are things in the programme office?'

'To be honest, it's a difficult working environment these days. Every couple of minutes young Derek suddenly squeaks 'Mazzarri Out!'

'Ah. A lot of people are saying that.'

'I don't think Derek means it, though. It just comes out. I think it's a sort of Tourette's Syndrome, brought on by distress at such monotonous football. And how are you faring yourself, Henry? I've noticed you slumped on the sofa a lot this week. You seem... troubled.'

Henry didn't want to admit how he was feeling. 'Oh, don't worry about me, old sport,' he said cheerily. 'I'm bright and breezy. Breezier than the East Stand after its roof was removed. Brighter than...'

Henry paused. He wanted to say he was feeling brighter than a certain season's home shirts. But he couldn't think which season. Nothing came to mind. For a man as besotted as Henry with kit colours and fabrics, this was serious. He realised he must be in a very dark place indeed. 'Golly,' he said. 'I... I think I need to talk things through, old fruit.'

'Of course, Henry. I'm here for you.'

'Thank you… But… Here's no good. What I've got to say feels too personal. I need to admit a few things.'

'I see. Well, maybe we could find a nice quiet game to revisit — where there won't be any Hornet Heaven residents in the crowd to overhear us. How about last weekend's game against Sunderland? No-one will be rushing back to watch that. Or the previous one — at Palace. Or the one before that — at home to Southampton. Or… Well, you get the idea.'

Henry thought for a second or two. Suddenly he knew the perfect place for confessing what was on his mind. He told Bill to stay where he was — and rushed down the slope of Occupation Road.

* * *

Not long later, Bill exclaimed: 'My old hut!'

Henry was standing next to a shabby red portacabin. He said: 'Yes. I've rebuilt it. I thought it would be a good place to—'

'The Bill Mainwood Programme Hut! I love my old hut. Where was it?'

'I found the walls lying in a stack beneath some overgrown brambles, down in the shadows where Lamper lurks.'

'My old hut! It reminds me of such happy days. The happy days before Watford's only aim was Premier League survival.'

'That's as maybe, old chap. But I've re-built the hut for a specific purpose.'

Bill wasn't really listening. He was stuck in a reverie. 'For me,' he said dreamily, 'it evokes an era when a mid-table team could have ambition. When there was always something to hope for. When the football wasn't so...' Bill came to his senses again. '...desperately, desperately boring.'

'Stop it, Bill! You're not helping!' Henry scolded. 'Come on, let's go inside.'

Henry ushered Bill through the door.

'Oh,' Bill said, disappointed. 'Where are all the programmes?'

'Ah. Yes. Well, I—'

'There's nothing of my old stuff here at all. Just two chairs and a curtain across the middle. I never had it arranged like this.'

Henry closed the door behind them and said: 'Look,

old thing. I need somewhere to… er… well, confess, I'm afraid. Would you mind sitting there? On the other side of this curtain?'

Bill went and sat on the far chair. Henry sat on the near chair.

Henry pulled the curtain between them and said: 'Forgive me, father, for I have sinned.'

'Wait a minute. *You're* The Father Of The Club. Shouldn't you be—'

'Bill! Please! I need you to do this for me.'

'Sorry, Henry. Of course.'

Bill cleared his throat and intoned solemnly: 'Watford be in your heart and upon your lips, my son, that you may truly and humbly confess your sins.'

Now Bill sat and listened as The Father Of The Club confessed what was on his mind.

'My disillusionment has caused my mind to turn to other things,' Henry said. 'Not just at this season's games. Even at the old games I go to.'

'Oh, dear.'

'Yes, It's awful. I've been to a lot of games from the 1990s recently, and I… Oh, dearie me… I've been… I've been trying to find a woman.'

'Find a woman? Henry Grover! Do you mean for

the purposes of… you know…?'

'Goodness me, Bill! I haven't been looking for *any* woman. I've been looking for a specific woman.'

'Oh. I see. And do you know her name?'

'Yes. Yes, I do. Her name's… Gladys Protheroe.'

'Gladys Protheroe?'

'Isn't it a gorgeous name? She sounds lovely. Similar age to me. Eighty. Just right. You know, Bill, I think… I think I've fallen a little in love.'

Bill knew exactly who Henry was talking about. Gladys Protheroe was famous among Watford fans for having turned eighty many, many times during the 1990s.

Henry continued: 'She was always being mentioned over the public address system at away games, but I've never been able to find her in the crowd.'

Bill knew there was a very good reason Gladys Protheroe couldn't be found. But he didn't say anything. He didn't want to break Henry's heart.

Henry said in a pained voice: 'I feel so guilty.'

'Of what, Henry? The sin of lust?'

'Far worse than that. Guilty that I'm letting down everyone in Hornet Heaven because my mind is elsewhere at times. I mean, what would The Big Fella say? What would The Great Man say?'

For a while, Bill let silence fill the hut as he wondered what to do. There was no point replying to Henry about Gladys Protheroe because Henry's feelings for Gladys Protheroe weren't the problem. They were merely a symptom of Henry's problem. And Bill knew exactly what Henry's problem was. He knew it because he was suffering from exactly the same thing himself.

Bill pulled back the curtain and helped The Father Of The Club to his feet. He said: 'Up you get, Henry.'

'Thank you for listening, Bill. I think it's helped.'

'Now sit there,' Bill said firmly.

'What?'

Bill pointed to where he'd been sitting and said: 'Sit there. It's my turn.'

They swapped seats. Bill drew the curtain between them. He began: 'Forgive me, father, for I have sinned.'

Henry was a bit surprised to find himself on the other side of the curtain listening to Bill confess.

Bill said mournfully: 'I live in an afterlife that contains nothing but football, but I'm not enjoying the football. And because of that, I've been starting to wonder whether... ...whether Hornet Heaven is actually the right place for me.'

Henry gasped. This was exactly how, deep down, he himself had been feeling. His search for Gladys Protheroe had been a way of avoiding addressing the existential question that he now realised had been gnawing away at him. He stood up and pulled back the curtain.

Bill looked up. Bill stood up.

The two men stared at each other, bonded by the recognition of what was troubling the deepest part of their souls.

'This is terrible!' Henry cried. 'Walter Mazzarri's football has got us questioning our very existence as Watford fans!'

Henry threw his arms round Bill.

Bill threw his arms round Henry.

They stood in each other's arms and wept for the certainty they'd lost.

* * *

Bill and Henry stepped out of the old hut and traipsed up the unusually grey Occupation Road, past the ancient turnstile. Up ahead, just outside the atrium, they saw Bill's assistant, 13-year-old Derek Garston, running towards them. He was waving a programme.

'Sir and Mr Grover, sir! Look! West Brom's in!'

Bill and Henry turned to each other. Neither felt in the mood to go to watch the latest Watford game.

'Come on, sir and Mr Grover, sir! It's under lights and everything! It could be one of those Vicarage Road nights, just like when The Great Man was manager!'

Bill and Henry didn't share Derek's optimism. But, reluctantly, they allowed Derek to press copies of the programme into their hands.

'Alright, then,' Henry sighed. 'If we must.'

They turned around and trudged back to the ancient turnstile, bracing themselves for more of Walter's torturous tedium.

* * *

Less than two hours later — after the final whistle — Bill and Henry's mood had transformed. They were up and dancing in the Rookery End, singing along to the song that was being played over the tannoy: 'Just Can't Get Enough' by Depeche Mode.

When the celebrations were over, the two men headed back towards the ancient turnstile with a spring in their steps.

Henry said: 'Good lord, Bill. Good lord. *That* is why we love football and Watford!'

'M'Baye Niang's goal!' Bill purred. 'Glorious!'

'His cross for Deeney's goal! Delicious!'

'Ten men hanging on for half an hour and not conceding!'

'Adrian Mariappa! One of our own! Playing like a titan!'

'All under the lights!'

*   *   *

When they emerged back onto Occupation Road, Henry noticed that the light was still abnormally grey. But his spirits weren't dampened. He said: 'You know, Bill. That performance was a very timely reminder of why we're in Hornet Heaven for eternity and would never want to be anywhere else — whatever temporary conditions may prevail.'

'Very true, Henry. That's exactly the thing about being a Watford fan. Somewhere along the line, there'll always be repayment for our staying true.'

They headed up the slope. Soon they saw Neil

McBain trudging towards them. Henry called out cheerily: 'Ah. Good evening to you, McBain. And what a fantastic evening it is!'

'What are you on about, Grover? Watford's football is ruining my afterlife,' McBain complained.

'Well, it's not ruining mine. We've just seen—'

Bill put his hand on Henry's arm to stop him. He said to McBain: 'We don't want to give you any spoilers, but you might want to go and watch the West Brom game.'

'Ach, it won't be worth it,' McBain replied. 'Even if the odd game's decent, it's never enough. The return on the overall investment just isn't there.'

Bill and Henry wondered if McBain was right. When they thought about it, tonight had definitely been good, but it was only the second time since early December that they'd come away from a game feeling glad they'd bothered. Their spirits began to sink again.

McBain continued: 'That's why I've decided I'm not going to any more of the new games.'

'What? Really?' Henry said. 'But won't you be bored on match days?'

'Less bored than if I watch the football.'

'But what will you do?'

'Ach, I'll go and watch an old game, I expect.'

'Oh dear. That's not good. You shouldn't spend your whole time living in the past, trying to ignore the present. That's what Luton fans do.'

Henry must still have been feeling a few last remnants of perkiness after what he'd seen against West Brom — because he was suddenly struck by a thought. He said to McBain:

'I say! Maybe your time as Luton manager in the 1930s made you a latent Luton fan!'

Bill Mainwood laughed. Neil McBain didn't.

'Ach, shut up about that! Let it lie! You're as bad as Harry Kent!'

Henry's perkiness was definitely returning. He chanted: 'Ooh, McBainy, Bainy! Used to be alright but he's a scummer now!'

Bill Mainwood laughed again. Neil McBain swore and stomped off.

Henry called out after McBain with a parting shot: 'Ha! A latent Luton fan, eh? Well, as I always say, "better never than latent"! Ha!'

After McBain had gone, Bill said to Henry: 'You shouldn't tease the man, Henry. He must be troubled enough already. Think about it. He's made the decision not to go and watch Watford when we're at the equal highest level in our history with the most expensive squad we've ever assembled. That would hurt any Watford fan.'

Henry sighed and replied: 'You're always so reasonable, Bill. But, come on. Surely we must be allowed to let a little light into our lives during the dark times. A game like tonight's against West Brom may have helped momentarily, but nothing brightens things up quite like thinking about the awful plight of our hapless rivals from up the road.'

Bill took a moment to check if this was actually true. He spent a few seconds reflecting how, over the last 10 seasons, Luton had managed to spend only 5 outside the lower divisions of the Football League — and how all of those were *below* the lower divisions of the Football League.

Bill giggled to himself.

Henry looked puzzled. 'What?' he asked.

'I'm thinking about Luton!'

Bill giggled some more.

'Oh no, Bill! Stop it! You're starting me off!'

Henry started giggling. Bill giggled even more. Henry ended up guffawing.

Eventually, Henry wiped the tears of laughter from his eyes and said with a sigh: 'Oh, Bill. No matter how bad the football gets at Watford, we'll always have Luton.'

Bill and Henry hugged each other again — happily this time. They felt a lot better than they had in Bill's hut. Maybe they'd lost perspective on how bad things actually were under Walter Mazzarri. Maybe they'd been infected by some kind of contagious mass negativity among Watford fans. Or maybe all they'd needed, all along, had been a backs-to-the-wall victory under the Vicarage Road lights — followed by a few Luton jokes. Who knew?

Bill said: 'I'll tell you what, though, Henry: I've learned something from this. As football fans, we often forget to count our blessings.'

Henry was just about to agree when there was a shout behind them.

'Oi! You two!'

Henry and Bill turned round. They saw Lamper, Hornet Heaven's chief steward, running up the slope of Occupation Road in his hi-vis jacket.

Henry greeted the former hooligan: 'Ah, Lamper. A very good day to you!'

Lamper replied: 'I don't know what you're so happy about. We've got an emergency down the road. A new arrival's refusing to come into Hornet Heaven!'

THE END

THE STORY CONTINUES IN
'GOING BACKWARDS'

7

GOING BACKWARDS

EARTH SEASON 2016/17

Lamper — a skinhead with violent tendencies who'd become Hornet Heaven's chief steward in 1980 — led Bill Mainwood and Henry Grover towards the ashen half-light of the lower reaches of Occupation Road. This was the limbo where new arrivals in Hornet Heaven materialised. Never before had a Watford fan refused to come in.

'The new arrival's a woman,' Lamper said. He sounded disappointed. 'Won't be much use as a scrapper.'

'A woman?,' Henry asked hopefully. 'Was her name Gladys, by any chance?'

'Henry!' Bill warned. 'Your mind's wandering again!'

'Gosh, old chap. So it is. Sorry. I'll, er… I'll start thinking up some Luton jokes in case we need them.'

They walked on. Soon, through the gloom, they saw the new arrival. She was leaning against the black stadium wall with her arms crossed in front of her 2016/17 home shirt.

Henry's heart began to flutter. But this clearly wasn't Gladys Protheroe. The woman in front of him was in her mid-twenties and had a very athletic figure.

'Good lord!' Henry said. 'I never thought this season's Dryworld shirt could have such… such élan!'

'Henry!' Bill hissed. 'Stop gawping and introduce us.'

'What? Oh. Yes. Hello. My name's Henry Grover. And this is Bill Mainwood. Welcome to Hornet Heaven.'

'No need to bother with all that,' the woman said. 'I'm not staying.'

Bill thought it would be a good idea to get the woman talking. He said: 'Well, it's always nice to meet another Watford fan — even briefly. At least tell us a little bit about yourself while you're here.'

The woman introduced herself as Kelly. She said she'd been born a supporter in 1992. She loved the Horns and was proud that Watford had become a Premier League club, but she didn't like what she was seeing this season. The terrible football on the pitch was a sign that the club's progress had stalled.

'A club has to keep moving forward,' she said, 'both on and off the pitch. But whenever Watford get the ball it's all sideways and backwards. Or we give it a big hoof upfield that sets the game back sixty years.'

'To be fair,' Bill said, 'we were a lot better against West Brom tonight.'

'A decent one-off performance won't cut it,' Kelly replied. 'We need the club to be on a permanent upward curve.'

'But how do you judge it? Standards in the Premier League are improving all the time. You need to keep getting better just to finish 17th each season.'

'You can't call it progress if you're narrowly avoiding relegation.'

'But we're doing more than that. We're 9th in the Premier League tonight.'

'You can't even judge it on league position. If we'd lost tonight, we'd have been 14th and staring over our shoulders. You have to look at the bigger picture to see whether the club is on the up. And it's obvious we aren't. Which means we'll be heading back down.'

'Oh dear.'

'Exactly. Not being in the Premier League doesn't bear thinking about — let alone living with for the rest of eternity.'

Lamper took the chance to speak up. He said: 'Nah, I reckon the club is definitely progressing. Loads of Watford fans are pissed off, so there's bound to be a bit of knuckle soon. Yeah, things look like getting much better, if you ask me.'

Henry interrupted. 'We won't be asking you, Lamper,' he said. 'Now. I'll tell you what, Kelly. I appreciate you're reluctant to commit to Hornet Heaven, but while you've popped in to see us, why don't you come and have a little look around? Go to an old game or two through the ancient turnstile. Maybe take one of Bill's… what do you call them, Bill?'

'Magical History Tours,' Bill said proudly.

'No thanks,' Kelly said. 'I don't care about the olden days. The Premier League — right here, right now — is the only place to be. If Watford aren't Prem, I don't want to watch at all.'

Bill looked at Kelly and scratched his head. His first impression of her was that she seemed very serious-minded. Briefly he wondered if he should take her on a tour of Watford's historic comedy moments: Pierre Issa falling off his stretcher, or Barry Endean dropping his shorts because Watford were going out of the cup, or Fernando Forestieri ploughing headfirst into a heap of snow.

Then a pressing existential question occurred to him. He asked: 'But what will you do instead if you decide not to come into Hornet Heaven?'

'I don't know,' Kelly answered. 'I suppose I'll just have to be satisfied that we survived two seasons in the Premier League for the first time ever — and let my soul be... I don't know... suspended in eternal nothingness.'

Bill thought this sounded rather bleak.

Henry leaned in and said: 'Suspended in eternal nothingness, eh, Bill? There's definitely a joke about being a Luton fan somewhere there. Do you want to do the honours or shall I?'

Bill felt the situation was a bit too heavy to be lightened with a Luton joke. He was about to start thinking up a plan when he was interrupted by Lamper — who'd got bored.

'Gawd! Hurry up and make your mind up, bird.'

Kelly stared at Lamper.

She said: 'Bird? Did you just call me bird?'

'Oh,' Lamper smiled. 'Don't like being called bird, bird? Want to make something of it, do ya?'

Kelly uncrossed her arms and went over to Lamper.

'Nice,' Lamper said. 'She wants a piece of me. Well, come and get it… bird!'

A moment later, Lamper was on the tarmac.

'Owwww!' he wailed. 'Not *that* piece of me! Owww! Right in the chutneys!'

Henry said: 'Golly, Kelly, you've got a lot of power in that right peg of yours. That reminded me of Matej Vydra's strike at home to Brentford in 2014.'

'Thanks.'

'But, listen. There's really no hurry for you to decide what to do. Spend a little time with us — there's no obligation.'

Kelly folded her arms again. Then she shrugged and unfolded them. She said: 'OK. I suppose so.'

Then she set off up the slope with Henry and Bill, being careful to tread on Lamper's hand.

* * *

A bit further up Occupation Road, Henry spotted Roy, from the IT department of Hornet Heaven.

'Ah, there you are, Roy!,' Henry said. 'Have you found out how to solve the lighting problem? Kelly, here, is just taking a look around and it would be nice for her to see our usual eternal sunshine. The place is getting as shadowy as Laurence Bassini's take-over.'

Roy nudged his glasses up his nose and said: 'Give me a chance, Henry. I've been busy on that other project you set me.'

'Ah. And how's that going?'

'Not well. You're asking me to alter history, and the post-2013 operating system won't let me do that.'

'But there must be a way. All I asked you to do was to stop the tannoy blaring out a particular song after the final whistle at home to Sunderland.'

Kelly asked: 'What song were they playing?'

Henry replied: ''That's Entertainment' — by The Jam. It was an affront. No-one could possibly describe that Sunderland game as entertainment.'

Henry harrumphed at the memory and let Roy continue on his way.

As Henry, Bill and Kelly carried on up the slope,

the two men discussed where they should take Kelly for her first game in Hornet Heaven. The mention of Sunderland got them quickly agreeing.

Bill popped into the atrium and picked up three programmes for Watford 8 Sunderland 0 on September 25th 1982.

*   *   *

Henry, Bill and Kelly went through the ancient turnstile and headed to the Vicarage Road end.

Kelly had never stood on an open terrace before. She discovered she loved it. Choosing where to stand made things feel much less regimented than in the Premier League. She loved the open skies above her head too. Everything seemed more natural — less of a carefully packaged product.

When the match started, Kelly watched, open-mouthed, as Watford poured forward from the kick-off. She saw fast, fearless, insistent attacking. The connection between the crowd and the team was electric — just because of the style of play. She'd seen clips of the game on YouTube before, but now she was experiencing how it actually felt to be part of it. It was as if everyone in the stadium was plugged into the same power source. It was intoxicating in a way that watching Watford this season had never been.

At half-time, with Watford 4-0 up, Kelly felt totally exhilarated.

But then she noticed Henry was gazing at her chest.

'Oi!' she said. 'What are you staring at?'

'Mmm? I do beg your pardon?'

'Enjoying a nice eyeful, are you?'

'Ah. Sorry. It's just that I wasn't a fan of the ladies' version of the home shirt when I saw it on a mannequin in the Hornets Shop. But in real life, it's quite magnificent. Superbly contoured.'

Kelly felt slightly flattered. But she wasn't going to show it. She said: 'You do know this isn't real life?'

'Absolutely. Hornet Heaven is much better than real life. I mean, think of the football you've just seen us playing. Barnes and Callaghan on the wings! Luther sprinting down the middle! Every time we get the ball it's exciting! It's a far cry from Wallyball.'

Kelly had to agree. But she knew the history of the Graham Taylor era. She said: 'This only lasted a few years during the 1980s. Then we were relegated when Bassett came in. All it does is remind me what happens if a club doesn't keep building and improving. I couldn't bear it if we weren't in the Premier League.'

Bill thought he could help. He said: 'Well, if you're frightened of relegation, maybe we ought to get you to confront your fear. In a nice way, of course.'

'Nice?' Kelly challenged. 'How can relegation ever be nice?'

'Ah. You never saw the 1974/75 season. It was the year we went down to Division Four. Come with us. You'll be surprised.'

* * *

Watford were playing Preston North End. It was the first home game of the 1974/75 league season. The Vicarage Road pitch was basking in brilliant sunshine.

Kelly noticed the stadium was less advanced than in 1982. There were no seats in front of the wooden Shrodells stand. There was a dog track between the pitch and the terracing. The place had character. Character of a kind that simply wasn't allowable in the Premier League.

When the match started, Bill pointed out some of the players.

'That's Mike Keen — the player/manager,' he said. 'He's in Hornet Heaven. Lovely man. And that little fellow is Denis Bond — our most impish midfielder ever. Though I'd need to get Derek to confirm the statistics on that, obviously. Denis is always a delight to watch. A beautiful footballer. He scores two goals today.'

Kelly watched as the Watford team passed the ball smoothly and swiftly, usually getting it out to the winger, Stewart Scullion. Scullion would receive the ball and immediately change direction. He'd lean like a motorcyclist rounding a bend at high speed, gliding smoothly past stationary defenders.

Suddenly Kelly recognised one of the Preston players that Scullion was breezing past.

'Wait! That's Bobby Charlton! Isn't he the best English player of all time?'

'He is,' Bill confirmed. 'And he can't get close to Scullion.'

Kelly kept watching. She couldn't take her eyes off Watford's football.

'This is brilliant stuff,' she said. 'How come we were relegated?'

'Oh, all kinds of reasons,' Bill replied. 'But,

looking back, I don't mind. We dropped into the bottom division, but we'll always have this football. It was gorgeous.'

Kelly thought this would be a lovely attitude to be able to have — not to care about divisional status. But it was the opposite of how she'd felt in the land of the living. Premier League status had underpinned everything she valued about being a Watford fan over the last couple of years.

'No,' she said. 'This is ignoring what's happening in the present day. I can't do that.'

Bill said: 'It's not ignoring the present day. It's providing context.'

'If the club goes backwards in 2017, it'll be a disaster,' Kelly argued. 'The TV money has made the stakes too high. Watford have to keep progressing — and it's obvious we aren't, because of the terrible football. I can't suddenly stop worrying about that.'

She paused and said apologetically: 'Look, thanks for trying, guys, but I'm sorry: the past isn't going to help me feel better about the present. I need to…' Suddenly she sounded defeated. 'I don't know what I need.'

Kelly turned and headed for the ancient turnstile.

Henry called out: 'Kelly! Don't go!'

'Sorry, Henry. It's just the way I am as a Watford fan.'

Henry and Bill watched Kelly go. Henry said: 'Oh dear, Bill. Why can't she see that the club *is* moving forwards?'

'Is it? Still?'

'Of course it is, old thing — in the grand scheme of things. When I founded the club in 1881, it was just a kick-around in Cassiobury Park. Perhaps we should force Kelly to go and watch all our matches, in order, from the start. Then she'd see how far we've come, and realise how fast we're hurtling into the future under Gino Pozzo.'

'We can't really force 5,000 matches on someone. But…'

Suddenly an idea struck Bill. '…Ooh!'

'Golly, Bill. Unless I'm very much mistaken, that sounded like an idea hatching. Do tell.'

Bill told Henry his idea. Henry thought it was brilliant.

'But… is it actually possible?' Henry asked.

'I don't know,' Bill replied. 'We'll have to ask Roy from IT. Let's go and find out.'

* * *

Kelly stepped despondently out of the ancient turnstile onto the sunless Occupation Road. She didn't know which way to turn. She looked around.

Coming down the slope was an elderly Watford fan with a moustache. He was chanting: 'Mazzarri Out! Mazzarri Out!'

Kelly had never studied ancient Watford history, so she didn't know that the man was Freddie Sargent — a forward from the first two decades of the club's existence. He was a cantankerous man who'd spent his life and afterlife protesting against things he didn't like — from professionalism in the 1890s to Jack Petchey a century later. The latest thing he didn't like was Walter Mazzarri.

Kelly did recognise the man who was walking up the slope towards Freddie, though. It was Mike Keen — the player/manager from the Preston game. He looked depressed.

Mike Keen said to Freddie Sargent: 'Less of the shouting, Freddie. Some of us here were sacked ourselves. From the club we love. Have a bit of consideration.'

'All managers are rubbish,' Freddie replied. 'We didn't have them in my day. We didn't need them. And this one's definitely got to go. Mazzarri Out! Mazzarri Out!'

Kelly was surprised to see antagonism between fans in Hornet Heaven. She'd always assumed that an afterlife paradise would be a place of never-ending harmony. Personally, she wasn't sure the current Head Coach deserved the abuse he was getting in the land of the living. But the fans' unhappiness was definitely more evidence, she reckoned, that the club's lack of progress was extremely hard to live with — on earth and in heaven.

After the two men had passed by, Kelly took in her surroundings. On one side of Occupation Road, the stadium's new black fascia was slick and stylish. On the other side was a brick garage. She moved towards the garage and noticed that the gnarled wooden planks of its doors were wearing the peeling remnants of a coat of mint green paint. It was a look an interior designer would call 'shabby chic'. Kelly could picture Henry Grover literally drooling over its weathered beauty. To be fair, she thought, it did look good in its own way. Just like Vicarage Road in 1974/75, it had character.

From the middle of the tarmac she could see that the two sides of Occupation Road represented Watford old and new. She guessed that the unmodernised garage might have been built in the 1920s, while the fascia had been added in 2015. But she didn't expect the fascia to remain unchanged for the next hundred years as the garage had done. At some point in the future it would start to look outdated. In which case, Watford's Premier League standards would mean the black and yellow scheme would be replaced and upgraded. The club had to keep moving forwards.

She stopped and thought. Would changing the black and yellow fascia really be moving forwards? It was just a veneer. Changing it would be cosmetic. Kelly frowned as a further thought occurred. Did this mean that the sign of progress she'd been hoping to see this season — better football — might only be superficial, rather than an actual advance?

Now her mind was whirring. Perhaps what she'd been wanting to see wasn't as fundamental as she'd thought. Perhaps there was something deeper that mattered more.

* * *

Later that day, Henry Grover found Kelly still on Occupation Road. He said: 'Ah, there you are. I've got something I want to show you.'

Henry walked her down the slope to the Bill Mainwood Programme Hut.

Kelly looked at the scruffy red portacabin. She reckoned it was halfway to being shabby chic, but only halfway. It was just shabby.

'I remember this horrible old thing,' she said.

'Shh, don't let Bill hear you say that,' Henry replied.

'What? He's not here. How could he hear me?

Henry quickly changed the subject. 'You see, the thing is,' he said, 'we've adapted the hut. A few days ago, I turned it into a confessional. But now we've refurbished it as... Well, in one way, it's like a fast-travelling time machine.'

'Ha! You mean the Bill Mainwood Programme Hut is now a Tardis?!'

'What? What's a Tardis? Is that something they have on earth now? You must remember I died in 1949.'

'Never mind. So what have you actually turned the

117

hut into?'

'It's a cinema. Roy in IT has downloaded every game from behind the ancient turnstile and made a time-lapse video of all the home games at Vicarage Road — from the very first one in 1922 onwards. It's brilliant. It takes you forward 95 years in time in just a few minutes. It means you can get an overview of Watford's progress without having to go to every single game.'

* * *

While Henry was explaining things to Kelly, Bill was with Roy in the IT office on an upper floor of the atrium. They were listening in to Henry and Kelly's conversation via a concealed microphone Henry was wearing.

'I can't believe she thinks my hut is horrible,' Bill complained. 'It would make a far better Tardis than some poxy police box.'

'Don't worry,' Roy replied. 'When she sees that your hut isn't just a normal cinema, but an IMAX cinema, she'll love it.'

'Well, I hope you're right. And I hope your video will convince Kelly to stay on in Hornet Heaven. During her time on earth, she only saw us progress from being a Championship club to being a Premier League club. Her lifetime was just a snapshot. The club's true growth over the years has been much more far-reaching — and now she's going to witness the whole of it. I hope it changes her perspective.

'Shh. I can hear her going into the hut. It's nearly time to start the video. Do you want to press the play button, or shall I?'

*   *   *

Down in the hut, Kelly stood in the exact middle of the floor.

Henry explained: 'It'll feel as if you're standing in the centre circle as the video plays on all four walls around you. Magnificent walls they are, too, actually. Vinyl-faced plasterboard, with a wipe-clean finish. Quite sumptuous.'

Kelly giggled. Henry re-focused his attention on the matter at hand.

'Yes. Well. Anyway,' he said. 'What you know as the Rookery End will be on that wall in front of you, and the Vicarage Road end will be behind you. The place will look very different to start with.'

Henry left the hut and Kelly tried to imagine what she was about to see. She couldn't visualise the stadium in 1922. But she assumed that the video would show various stands going up as Vicarage Road became an all-seater Premier League stadium. Not long ago, she'd seen an excellent time-lapse video of the Sir Elton John stand being built over the course of a few months. She reckoned a similar video, over 95 years, would be pretty amazing.

* * *

Up in the IT office, Bill pressed the button to play the video. He said: 'There we go. Perfect. Everything's gone to plan.'

Roy said: 'Yup. It's all… Hang on. What have you done?'

'I pressed the button you told me to press.'

'Oh no! This isn't right!'

'What? What's wrong?'

'I don't know how this is happening.'

'What's happening? Tell me what's happening.'

'The time-lapse video is playing backwards. It's

starting in 2017. It'll end up in 1922 — when Vicarage Road was a recently converted gravel pit!'

'Oh golly! This is a disaster! It's showing her the *opposite* of progress!

Bill rushed out of the IT office as fast as he could.

* * *

Kelly stood in the hut and watched as the Sir Elton John stand was unbuilt and a derelict East Stand rose from the ground. It wasn't pretty.

But things started to look better when a roof appeared on the East Stand. The old thing, in its day, definitely had personality, she thought.

Before long, the Rookery and Vicarage Road stands vanished. At the Vicarage Road end a vast sweep of terracing appeared. Then the Rous stand sank into the ground and the small yellow Shrodells stand arose in its place. Kelly loved its unsophisticated charm.

The video was moving fast. It was a lot for Kelly to take in, this unpeeling of the Vicarage Road she knew. But she liked it. It reminded her of the time, back on earth, that she'd been stripping wallpaper and found some amazing old fabric on the walls underneath. This felt the same. As if valuable hidden treasure was being revealed.

The video came to an end and she turned 360 degrees on the spot, taking in what Vicarage Road was like in 1922. Earth banking. Small boxy stands. Telegraph poles. Trees. It definitely wasn't Premier League. It was beautiful.

* * *

On Occupation Road, Bill ran down the slope towards the hut. 'Oh dear! Oh dear!' he panted.

He looked ahead and saw Henry. He called out: 'It's all gone terribly wrong! We've shown her Watford going backwards!'

He arrived at the hut, scarcely able to breathe. He bent forward, with a hand on Henry's shoulder for support, and tried to gasp some air into his lungs.

Then, when he looked up, he saw Kelly emerging from the hut. She was grinning. She said: 'That was amazing!'

Bill was stunned.

'What? Really?'

'Totally. I loved it. By stripping everything back to

1922 you showed me how much soul Vicarage Road has
— how much soul the club has. It was all there beneath
everything I'd thought was the important stuff. Thank
you.'

'Oh… Well… You're very welcome.'

Henry said: 'Goodness me, old thing. Well done.'

'Er, thank you, Henry. Quite a masterstroke in the
end.'

'In fact, old chap, do you know what? I'd rather like
to see this video myself. Given what I was saying when
we were using the hut as a confessional, I think I
probably rather need it.'

'Good idea. Me too.'

Through his microphone, Henry asked Roy to play
the video backwards again, and the two men went inside
the hut.

Kelly hurried in behind them to watch the video
again. Not only had it persuaded her to continue being a
Watford fan for the rest of eternity, but it was the most
watchable thing she'd seen at Vicarage Road since
Manchester United at home back in September.

* * *

Over the next few weeks, Kelly went back to watch old Watford games all day every day. Meanwhile, the 2017 team went back to playing unimaginative and uninspired football. They lost 4 of their next 5 matches, scoring only one goal. During that time, the backwards time-lapse video proved hugely popular. There was always a huge queue at the door of the hut. In the subdued light, the queue snaked up Occupation Road, past the barely used ancient turnstile, all the way to the atrium. Bill and Henry attributed the video's success to the fact that it was the only new footage in Hornet Heaven that made you feel good.

On May 12th, the programme for the away game at Everton came in. As Henry and Bill walked down Occupation Road on their way to the match, they saw that people were choosing to queue for repeat viewings of the video rather than going to an actual Watford game.

Bill said: 'Well, I suppose it tells us something about supporting a football team. Re-tracing your steps to the beginning can make you feel a lot happier about where you've got to so far.'

'Absolutely, old fruit,' Henry agreed. 'It definitely worked for Kelly. You know, it still feels good that she deliberately chose to remain a Watford fan for the rest of eternity, come what may. It definitely put an end to my own doubts.'

Suddenly they heard a shout behind them.

'Oi! You two!'

Henry and Bill turned round. It was Lamper again.

'Blinking flip!' Lamper said. 'It's one crisis after a bleeding nother. First a newbie didn't want to come in. Now there's a bloke who's been here for years who wants to quit Hornet Heaven! He wants to end it all!'

THE END

THE STORY CONTINUES IN
'A WORLD WITHOUT BEAUTY'

8

A WORLD WITHOUT BEAUTY

EARTH SEASON 2016/17

The Hornet Heaven resident who wanted to end it all was searching for an exit where new arrivals entered — in the drab twilight of the lower reaches of Occupation Road. Henry and Bill wanted to help him, so, instead of going to the away game at Everton, they followed Lamper down into the gloom.

Bill asked: 'Is he in a very bad way, Lamper?'

'Not as bad as he will be if he don't cheer up soon. I'll lamp him one, good and proper.'

'Now, now, Lamper,' Bill said. 'This is a time for compassion, not threats of violence.'

'But he's gettin' right on my tits!'

'Lamper! At moments like this you need to be more sensitive.'

'My tits are very sensitive!'

Henry intervened and put an avuncular arm around Lamper's shoulders. He said: 'The thing is, Lamper, we need to show a bit more understanding. This is a man who no longer wants to live. Or no longer wants to be dead. Or something. Either way, this is a man who wants to end his afterlife.'

'Well, I suppose when you put it like that…'

'Exactly. It's a terribly serious matter. We need to consider very carefully how we're going to handle the situation.'

There was a short silence. Then Lamper said: 'Shall I think up some Luton jokes?'

'That'll be perfect,' Henry replied.

* * *

Soon, in the murk, Henry and Bill saw the outline of a man sitting hunched on the kerb, with his head on his knees in despair. Lamper said: 'Here he is. I told him to clear off back to Hornet Heaven proper. I kicked him a few times too. I enjoyed that. But he won't budge. He's your problem now.'

Lamper disappeared into the shadows.

Henry still couldn't make out who the man was. He went and sat on the kerb next to the distressed figure. He said: 'Hello. I'm The Father Of The Club. I'm hoping I can help you.'

The man said: 'Leave me alone. No-one can help me. I want out.

Henry recognised the voice immediately: 'I say, is that you, Mike?'

Mike Keen, Watford's manager from the mid-1970s, nodded despondently. 'Yes, it's me,' he said. 'But not for long. I've always been committed to the ideal of beautiful football. And since Walter Mazzarri isn't even trying to play attractively, I'd rather not be here. I don't want to live in a world without beauty.'

Bill sat down on the kerb on the other side of Mike. He said: 'Oh dear, Mike. It must be especially awful for you. You gave us some gorgeous football during your time as manager. Remember Preston?'

A huge sob burst out of Mike Keen.

'Oh,' Bill said. 'Sorry.'

Henry looked at the downcast former boss and remembered how he and Bill had managed to lift themselves out of their pit of despair after the Sunderland game. He was confident he already had the answer to the problem. He decided to waste no time.

He said: 'You know, Mike. Bill and I were feeling exactly the same way as you about the tripe we've been watching. And do you know what? The thing that cheered us up was the knowledge that in Hornet Heaven, at least our afterlives aren't tainted by anything to do with Luton!'

Henry frowned.

'Ah... Oh dear... Mike?... Are you alright?'

Mike Keen had slumped forward and was lying on the tarmac in a foetal position.

Bill said: 'Ah. I've just remembered. Mike played over 100 games for Luton before he joined us. It's a mistake that has always rather haunted him.'

'Ah,' Henry said. 'Bugger.'

* * *

Mike Keen felt himself being carried up Occupation Road by his arms and legs. The light, further up the slope, was unusually grey, but Mike felt a greater darkness pressing down on his mind.

He'd always believed in beautiful football. In the 1970s, he'd played with elegance in Watford's midfield, and he'd encouraged the same from his players when he became manager. It wasn't about aesthetics. It was about principle. Any team could play ugly football. A good team should always reach for a higher plane.

The darkness that was pressing down on his mind was that Watford were a good team, but weren't playing like a good team. Technically, the squad contained better players than the club had ever possessed. But their attacking football was lumpy-humpy. It hurt the eyes and the soul.

And now he was being carried back to the heart of Hornet Heaven to be made to watch more of it.

He tried to kick out, to free himself, but he just didn't have the strength.

* * *

In the atrium, Bill and Henry laid the former manager down on one of the yellow leather sofas. They stepped back and watched him try to doze.

Bill said: 'The current dissatisfaction with the Head Coach can't be helping him, either. All the shouts of

'Mazzarri Out!' must bring back very painful memories. When Mike was manager, Watford fans chanted for *his* dismissal.'

'Goodness,' Henry said. 'I remember that! How did it go? Keen Out! Keen Out! That was great fun.'

Mike Keen's limbs began twitching helplessly.

Bill scolded Henry for his insensitivity and knelt down next to Mike. He held Mike's hand and said: 'I'm so sorry to see you like this, Mike. Perhaps we should take you to tonight's game at Everton in the hope that Watford's performance will give you reason for living.'

Henry interrupted: 'Huh! Fat chance!'

Mike just shook his head weakly and murmured: 'I can't go on as a Watford fan.'

Bill patted Mike's hand and wondered how they could help him. Merely bringing him back up to the atrium clearly wasn't going to be enough.

Bill got to his feet. He announced to Henry: 'Right. This man needs treatment. As a matter of urgency. He needs a specialist.'

'Right,' Henry said. 'Of course. But... What kind of specialist?'

Bill knew exactly who could help Mike.

He said: 'This is another job for Roy in IT.'

* * *

Henry and Bill carried Mike Keen by the arms and legs again. They headed down through the strangely dim light of Occupation Road towards Bill's old hut.

Henry said: 'You know, Bill, I'm very glad I rebuilt your hut. It's proved awfully useful. First a confessional, then an IMAX cinema, and now an emergency clinic.'

Kelly, the recent arrival in Hornet Heaven, was waiting for them at the hut. She'd put up a sign on the portacabin door. The sign had a medical-looking symbol on it — a red cross on a yellow background. This caused a brief argument between Henry and Bill about whether the cross should have been red or black.

Kelly said: 'Don't squabble, boys. Roy says Mike's treatment is ready. I hope it works. The man who gave Watford fans that Preston game in 1974/75 doesn't deserve to be suffering like this.'

Kelly left, and Henry and Bill carried Mike into the hut. The former manager seemed barely conscious.

They stretched Mike out on a trolley. Bill said gently: 'We're going to make you feel well again.'

Mike lay on his back and nodded feebly.

Henry and Bill rolled the trolley backwards until Mike's head was inside a machine that looked just like the MRI scanner at Watford General Hospital.

Bill said: 'Just open your eyes a little and look straight up.'

Henry gave a signal to Roy through his microphone, and footage started to play on the curved surface above Mike's head. Mike peered at it, dead-eyed.

There was snow around the edge of the Vicarage Road pitch. Almen Abdi brought the ball down in Watford's half and played it forward to Fernando Forestieri on the halfway line. Fessi touched it back to Jonathan Hogg, and Hogg returned it to Fessi. Fessi took the ball towards the Rous stand and pushed it out to Lloyd Doyley. Doyley moved it on to Marco Cassetti on the touchline. Cassetti played it first time, square, to Fessi who dummied it for Cristian Battochio. Battochio exchanged swift passes, twice, with Almen Abdi, back and forth. Then, as Battochio sprinted forward, Abdi passed forward to Fessi — who let the ball run on to Cassetti again, further up the touchline. Cassetti curled the ball deliciously along the ground into the path of Battochio, on the edge of the box. Battochio, with an exquisite touch, redirected the ball into the Huddersfield goal, just inside the far post.

Mike's eyelids flickered. The slightest of sparkles began to light his eyes. The footage, on loop, now showed Abdi bringing the ball down again at the start of the move.

Henry and Bill watched Mike. Bill murmured: 'It's working! The acute treatment is working!'

Mike watched the goal time and time again. Soon his eyes were shining. He was sighing with pleasure at the beauty of what he was watching.

Henry, The Father Of The Club, watched the former manager's reaction. He found himself welling up. Thanks to a timely emergency intervention, Mike Keen was back from the brink.

* * *

On the Sunday, for some peace and quiet after so much stress recently, Henry headed to the Sensory Room in the north east corner of the stadium.

When he arrived, the main section overlooking the pitch was empty. But there was someone in the Calming Area. It was Freddie Sargent. Henry found his old team-mate from the 1880s reclining on a yellow beanbag, massaging his temples and gazing silently at a wall projection of an aquarium. He said: 'Hello, Freddie.'

Freddie looked a bit unsettled by the interruption. He diverted his attention to beads of air rising up a bubble tube.

'Been to any decent games recently?' Henry asked.

Freddie, like many fans, felt that Watford didn't really do decent games any more. He started to look cross. He picked up a yellow cushion in the shape of Harry The Hornet's face and started stroking it.

'Good idea, old son,' Henry said. 'I think we could all do with a bit of comfort. Especially after Friday's toothless defeat at Everton.'

Freddie could stand it no longer. He said: 'Gah! For God's sake, Henry, shut up about the football! I'm trying to stay calm!'

'Oh dear. Sorry, Freddie. Has something been getting your goat?'

'Not something. Someone. Walter bloody Mazzarri. He totally winds me up. Doesn't speak English. Doesn't wave to the fans.'

'Ah. I see. Well, you're probably wise to spend time in here trying to restore your inner peace. I mean, Walter has led us to six away defeats in a row.'

The statistic incensed Freddie. He punched Harry The Hornet's face and shouted: 'Gah! I hate Mazzarri! I just hate him!'

'Oh dear, Freddie. Hate's a strong emotion. Are you sure—'

'I can't help it! It's how I feel!'

Freddie took a few deep breaths and said: 'Right. Leave me alone. I'm going to try and centre myself by contemplating the glitter ball on the ceiling here.'

As Freddie settled back into his beanbag, hugging the Harry The Hornet cushion, Henry's attention was drawn by the changing coloured lights that were embedded in the fibre-optic carpet. The way they were fading in and fading out reminded him of Etienne Capoue.

He said: 'I suppose the buck does have to stop with Walter. After all, we haven't even scored a goal in the last six away games. In fact, Bill's young assistant Derek calculated that we've been goal-less for 10 hours and 17 minutes of football away from home. He said that, mathematically, at the current rate, we won't score for the rest of eternity.'

The extra statistics made Freddie lose all control. He yelled: 'Arrrrgghh! Boooooo! Boooooo! Mazzarri

Out! Mazzarri Out!'

At the end of the outburst, Freddie buried his face into Harry The Hornet's and let out a muffled whimper.

Henry watched. He didn't know what to do. He patted Freddie on the shoulder and said: 'Good man, Freddie. Good man. Best try and keep a lid on it, old son.'

Awkwardly, he sidled backwards out of the Calming Area.

When he turned, he bumped into someone. It was Lamper.

'Oi!' Lamper said. 'I oughta stick one on you!'

'What? Why?'

'Hiding in here when you're needed.'

'I'm not hiding. What's happened now?'

'It's that bleeding Mike Keen again. He wants to leave Hornet Heaven! Again!'

* * *

Henry left Freddie Sargent in the Calming Area and returned to the nether regions of Occupation Road. This time, in the gloom, Mike Keen looked totally wired. His hands had developed a tremor. His pupils were dilated.

Henry said: 'Lummee, Bill. What's happened to the man?'

Bill had taken it upon himself to supervise Mike, trying to keep the former manager safe. He said: 'I think we gave him too high a dose of the emergency treatment in my hut. He's become addicted to Zola's football.'

Henry sighed and said: 'Ah. Weren't we all, for a short glorious while.'

Bill continued: 'Ever since the treatment, he's spent the whole time watching every single Zola match back-to-back. Now he can't get enough.'

'Well, it was rather more-ish,' Henry said.

Mike came over to Henry. He seized Henry's lapels and demanded: 'More Zola! I need more Zola!'

Mike let go and went off to rattle a stretch of rusty fencing in his search for the exit.

'Well,' Henry said, 'this is a very poor show, I must say. It's terribly irresponsible of Mike to binge on so much Zola in such a short period.'

'I agree,' Bill said. 'Mike may well have strong principles about beautiful football, but excessive indulgence in it — out of context — is mind-altering. It makes you forget that football has to meet objectives — and Zola didn't succeed in getting us promoted from the

Championship. The football wasn't up to its task.'

'But I don't understand why Mike's trying to leave Hornet Heaven. There's plenty of delicious Zola behind the ancient turnstile.'

Mike was now delving through brambles, mumbling to himself: 'Fresh Zola. I must have fresh Zola.'

Bill said: 'He's heard Gianfranco's been at Birmingham City this season, so he wants to go to *their* Heaven.'

'Golly. Are you sure a club like Birmingham would have a heaven?'

'No idea. If it does, young Derek suggested it would be called "Bluenose Bliss".'

Henry watched as Mike continued showing all the signs of addiction to a drug as powerful as Zola's football: unusual excitement, euphoria and intense cravings. Henry felt a little jealous that none of these sensations had been available to Watford fans under Walter Mazzarri. Attractive football had been a strictly controlled substance.

'Right, then,' Henry said. 'Mike clearly needs help. Any ideas?'

'I'm going to refer him to a specialist.'

'Oh, golly. I hope you don't mean Roy in IT again. Success can't be achieved by simply repeating something that hasn't worked. Did watching Aidy Boothroyd's hoofball teach you nothing?'

'I mean a different specialist, Henry. This is a job for someone who knows all about addiction. We need a man who used to stop the team coach at a pub so he could get a drink. A man who was sacked for misappropriating club monies to fund his gambling.'

'My goodness, Bill. You're right. This is a job for Neil McBain.'

*　　*　　*

Henry found Neil McBain in the atrium. He was encouraged when Watford's manager from the 1930s and 1950s agreed to help.

Henry said: 'You know all about addiction, McBain. What's the secret of getting someone like Mike to pull himself together?'

McBain replied: 'Well, I'm old school, Henry. I believe in tough love.'

'Ah. I've never quite understood that phrase. What does it mean?'

'Tough love means harsh treatment that's good for someone in the long run because there's love behind it.'

'How interesting. Harsh treatment seems to be Walter Mazzarri's management style. Maybe it'll prove good for the players in the long run.'

'I said there has to be love behind it.'

'Ah. Good point.'

*   *   *

Very soon, Mike Keen found himself following Neil McBain along Occupation Road towards the ancient turnstile. He said: 'You've got to help me, McBain. I live for beautiful football. I need another fix.'

'Stick with me,' McBain replied, 'and I'll sort you out.'

'Sort me out with some Zola? Oh, thank you. I love you, man.'

'Ach, get off me. I mean sort you out once and for all. I've chosen a game for us to go to. From 1974/75.'

Mike's eyes widened in anticipation. His voice quavered as he said: 'At home to Preston? Wow. That's serious stash.'

McBain took Mike Keen through the ancient

turnstile. They arrived on the night of Tuesday April 29th 1975.

'Not Preston,' McBain said. 'Walsall at home. The final game of the season.'

Mike's eyes hollowed in horror. He said: 'But that's the night….'

'The night we were relegated into the bottom division,' McBain confirmed. 'Come on, you need to see this. There's a harsh lesson you need to learn about beautiful football.'

* * *

Mike watched Watford line up against Walsall under the floodlights. Mike recalled the stakes: all Watford needed to do was win and they'd stay up. He suddenly felt sober.

Watford were in their mid-1970s kit: yellow shirts with two black vertical stripes running down from the left shoulder. Mike thought the kit looked extremely stylish, but he couldn't remember how stylishly the team had played in tonight's 3-2 defeat. He'd never been back to find out. Now he was here, though, he hoped to see that his team had remained a credit to his footballing principles.

He followed McBain to the Vicarage Road terrace. As the match kicked off, he looked around. The fans looked anxious. Fearful. He listened to what they were shouting. It was a single game that could save Watford from relegation and they weren't baying for beautiful football. They were yelling for effort and commitment. Mike dreaded to think what that might make the football look like.

After a while, Walsall took the lead. Mike winced. He said to McBain: 'I know we went down, but we had players capable of some fantastic stuff. Look at them out there: Denis Bond, Stewart Scullion, Bobby Downes.'

'And tell me,' McBain replied, 'did their beautiful football keep us in the division?'

Mike knew it was a rhetorical question, but he couldn't help answering: 'It should have done.'

As soon as the words left his lips, he began to recognise the state of denial he'd been in for the 42 years since tonight's events.

As the match progressed, Watford couldn't seem to get a foothold in the game. The fans around Mike seemed to get more and more anxious as relegation loomed larger. They shouted for the players to get the ball into the box. Mike shook his head sadly.

'I wanted us to keep trying to play beautiful football.'

This seemed to annoy McBain. The Scotsman said: 'Ach, Mike. It's time to face facts. The problem wasn't prettiness. The problem was defending.'

'I know, but—'

'Listen to me. Here's the truth. If you'd stopped one of Preston's two goals the previous Tuesday and just one of Walsall's three tonight, Watford would have got two more points and stayed up. Preventing two goals was all it would have taken. However ugly it might have looked.'

Mike stared down at the terrace, processing this.

McBain finished by saying: 'Beautiful football is never the answer in a survival situation.'

Mike Keen lifted his eyes to the night sky. He knew, deep down, that what McBain was saying was true. It was just that, for all of his footballing life and afterlife, he hadn't wanted it to be true.

Mike turned to leave.

McBain said: 'Oh no you don't. You're staying. You need to experience the evening in full. For your own good.'

When the final whistle went, Watford were relegated to Division Four. Back in 1975, Mike hadn't hung around to see what had happened. Now, from the terrace, he saw there was a pitch invasion. Fans wearing flared trousers and platform shoes strode onto the pitch, fists clenched, eyes blazing. Most were chanting 'Bonser Out!'. But some were chanting 'Keen Out!'.

This time, when he heard the chant, Mike didn't twitch helplessly. Instead he nodded.

At last he recognised that the relegation had been his fault. He'd been trying to play the wrong kind of football. He should have played whatever kind of football might have stopped this happening. He'd got it terribly wrong. Anything was better than the pain of Watford being relegated.

And anything included Walter Mazzarri's football in 2017.

* * *

Two days later, after Watford's final away defeat of the season, at Chelsea, Henry Grover and Bill Mainwood were relaxing on the yellow leather sofas in the atrium. Mike Keen came and sat down with them.

145

Henry said: 'Ah. Mike. I hear McBain did an excellent job with you.'

'He did,' Mike replied. 'He taught me that we can't always expect to see beautiful football. There's a reason Walter has had us playing the lumpy-humpy stuff.'

'So, from now on,' Henry asked with a note of mischief in his voice, 'can we expect to hear you shouting Mazzarri In?'

'I don't know about that. But it did make me think something that Freddie Sargent isn't thinking when he shouts Mazzarri Out. I'm thinking: Walter Mazzarri is clearly a better coach than me.'

Bill asked: 'And how are things now, Mike? Are you bearing up?'

'I went to Stamford Bridge. We played some decent stuff for once. Janmaat's dribble into the box for his goal was superb.'

'It must have reminded you of Stewart Scullion against Preston.'

'It didn't. I've learned not to idealise beautiful football any more. The most important thing about the trip to Chelsea was discovering that we were mathematically safe from relegation. We've survived in the Premier League again. Which means that Walter's unadventurous approach was justified. It did its job.'

Henry and Bill were both pleased to hear that Mike's new perspective had allowed him to find a way out of the misery he'd been in.

Bill said: 'So are you planning to stay in Hornet Heaven now?'

Henry added mischievously again: 'You're not going to do what so many Watford fans did at games this season and leave early?'

'I'm sticking with it,' Mike said. 'The summer's nearly here and I'm hoping we can all wipe the slate clean. I think we need to accept that Mazzarri did what he had to do to keep us in the Premier League for only the second time ever, and get ready to go again next season.'

Henry and Bill both nodded. After so many recent troubles — their own crisis, Kelly's doubts, and Mike's despair — they were optimistic that everyone in Hornet Heaven would now be much more emotionally stable.

Suddenly, though, they heard Derek Garston running into the atrium.

'Sir and Mr Grover, sir! Sir and Mr Grover, sir!'

Bill said: 'Goodness, young man. What's going on?'

'It's an emergency, sir! One of the residents is on the roof of the Sir Elton John Stand, sir! I'm frightened he's going to jump!'

THE END

THE STORY CONCLUDES IN
'ONE MAN ALONE'

9

ONE MAN ALONE

EARTH SEASON 2016/17

On the left-hand side of the Hornets Shop, Henry Grover and Bill Mainwood set about trying to clamber up the wall adjoining the Sir Elton John stand. They were racing to save the man on the roof.

92-year-old Bill gave 83-year-old Henry a leg-up. Henry reached up to the edge of the roof and called out: 'I can't quite get a finger-hold, Bill. It's just like the Premier League used to be.'

Bill got a better grip under Henry's boot and said: 'One last effort, Henry. On the count of three.'

'Wait. Three is Miguel Britos. We need to summon up the strength and spirit of Troy Deeney. Count to nine.'

Bill counted to nine and heaved Henry higher than before. Henry grabbed the edge of the roof and hauled himself up. Then he reached down and hauled Bill up. They ran south along the roof towards the centre of the Sir Elton John Stand.

Ahead of them, a figure was crouched on the edge of the roof looking down over Occupation Road. Henry recognised immediately who it was. It was Freddie Sargent, the former Watford Rovers striker who had died in 1942.

Henry shouted: 'Freddie! Don't do it, old son!'

Freddie Sargent turned. He saw Bill and Henry rushing towards him. 'Leave me alone,' he growled. 'You won't stop me. Walter Mazzarri has driven me to this.'

Bill and Henry came to a halt a few yards away from Freddie. They didn't dare go closer.

Bill said cautiously: 'Come on, Freddie, let's talk this over.'

'There's nothing to discuss,' Freddie replied. 'Mazzarri's not going to change his ways.'

'But honestly, Freddie. That's no reason to throw yourself off the roof.'

Freddie peered over the edge. 'If I did go over,' he said, 'I'd be in free fall. Just like Watford for the last few weeks.'

'Please, Freddie! Step back! You're terrifying young Derek down there!'

'Nothing's more terrifying than the prospect of Mazzarri staying.'

Freddie leant even further forward over the edge of the roof.

'No! Don't do it! You'll kill yourself!'

'I wonder if there's an after-afterlife? If there is, and Mazzarri's still manager, and I killed myself again, would there be an after-after-afterlife?'

Freddie transferred his weight back onto the roof. He had something in his hands now. He held it out towards Henry and Bill.

'Don't be stupid. I'm not jumping. I'm hanging up this banner so everyone on Occupation Road can see it.'

Freddie was holding a yellow banner daubed with huge black letters. It said 'Mazzarri Out!'.

'Oh, thank goodness!' Bill sighed. 'Thank goodness!'

Bill and Henry felt a wave of relief pass through them. They sank down onto the roof and sat quietly until they'd recovered.

After a while, Bill said: 'Well, I have to say, Freddie, I find that banner of yours completely inappropriate. Wouldn't you agree, Henry?'

'Absolutely, old thing. That black lettering definitely ought to be red.'

For a minute or so, Bill and Henry had their usual squabble about red versus black.

Then Bill said: 'Anyway. What I meant is, I think it's unreasonable for fans to put all the blame on the Head Coach. The team's troubles are a complex situation arising from multiple causes.'

Freddie wasn't in a mood to debate. He'd been passionate about Watford Football Club for more than 100 years, and it was passion that was driving his feelings about Walter Mazzarri.

'Our problems are down to one man alone,' he said. 'I hate him. I just want him gone.'

'But the fortunes of football clubs never depend on a single man,' Bill replied. 'Right now there are all kinds of things combining to make fans angry. There's the problem of being a mid-table Premier League club. There are expectation levels that are too high. Isn't that right, Henry?'

Henry wasn't really concentrating on what Bill was saying. He'd heard something about a single man, which had reminded him he was a single man himself in Hornet Heaven, which had got him thinking romantic thoughts about Gladys Protheroe again.

'What?. . Oh. I, er… To be honest, Bill, I'm finding what you're saying rather befuddling. What do *you* think, Freddie?'

Freddie lifted up the banner. Henry read it again.

'Ah. Yes. There. Much better. You see, I understand that, Bill. Two words. Mazzarri Out! It's so much simpler. Right. I've decided. I'm with Freddie.'

'But it's not a simple issue, Henry. As I say, the fortunes of football clubs don't revolve around one man.'

'No. I'm sorry, old thing, but I've made up my mind.'

Henry got up. He went over to Freddie and took hold of one end of the banner.

'But this is completely unjust,' Bill complained. 'The Head Coach has done his job. He's kept us in the Premier League.'

Henry started to help Freddie hang the banner from the edge of the roof. He said: 'The thing is, Bill, I don't

153

want to spend the whole of eternity having to rescue people like Kelly, Mike Keen and even ourselves from spiritual crisis. Sacking the Head Coach is an easy solution.'

'But an easy solution is rarely the correct solution.'

When Henry said nothing, Bill realised he'd lost the argument up here on the roof. He watched as Freddie and Henry leaned down over the edge of the roof and unfurled a banner that pinned all of the fans' current upset on a man who'd led Watford to their seventh best league finish in history.

Bill galvanised himself. He felt strongly about the matter. He may have lost an ally in Henry, but he had plenty more potential allies in Hornet Heaven.

He got up and headed back along the roof towards the atrium to recruit someone else who could help him win the argument.

* * *

Before he did anything else, Bill popped into the programme office to reassure Derek that Freddie wasn't planning to leap off the roof after all.

'Thank goodness, sir,' Derek said. 'My efforts paid

off, then, sir.'

'Really? What efforts were those, young man?'

'I summoned up the spirit of a player to help the situation, sir.'

'Aha. Was it Troy Deeney, by any chance?'

'No, sir. It was Simon Sheppard. He played in goal for us between 1992 and 1994.'

'That's a strange choice, my boy. How would that have helped?'

'Simon Sheppard was no good at jumping, sir. Which is never much use for a goalkeeper, but very handy for people on a roof.'

Bill frowned. Sometimes, he felt, the boy got some strange notions into his head.

Bill moved the conversation on. He said: 'We've still got a problem with Freddie, though. He's very worked up. He can't see past blaming everything on one person — which is terribly unjust. So I'm just off to ask a few people for ideas on how to change that. I'll see you later.'

Bill started to leave the office.

'Wait a moment, sir. If you want to calm Freddie down, I've got a great idea.'

Bill suspected this might be another of Derek's

strange notions. He carried on walking and said: 'No thanks, young man. All I need is a way to stop Freddie thinking Walter Mazzarri is the cause of all our woes.'

'But my idea would put your hut to another new use, sir.'

'No, Derek, I don't need—'

'But you wouldn't want a hut with your name on it sitting idle, sir, would you, sir? That would give a terrible impression, sir.'

Bill stopped in the doorway. 'Well, when you put it like that, young man… OK. But don't do anything I wouldn't do.'

Then Bill went off to find someone who could help him nip Freddie Sargent's 'Mazzarri Out' campaign in the bud.

* * *

By the programme shelves in the atrium, Bill found Neil McBain.

After McBain's recent success in helping Mike Keen come to terms with Watford's awful football, Bill reckoned Watford's former manager from the 1930s and 1950s was just the man he needed. He said: 'I'm after your help, McBain. Freddie Sargent is campaigning for Walter Mazzarri to be sacked, and I want to persuade him that it's unfair to blame the gaffer.'

'Ach, it's always unfair to blame the gaffer,' McBain replied.

'Good. I'm glad you think that. You and I will make a great team on this.'

'People are always prejudiced against the boss. I mean, everybody thinks I was a failure as Watford's manager.'

'Yes. Twice.'

'Watch it, Mainwood. Don't rub it in.'

'Sorry.'

'Like I say, everybody thinks I was a failure as Watford's manager — but all the problems were due to aspects beyond my control.'

'I agree. But do you reckon you could prove what you're saying to Freddie Sargent?'

'Of course. All I'd have to do is take him back to the 1957/58 season.'

'When we were relegated?'

'Aye. Relegation's what I get blamed for. But we finished ninth from bottom in Division Three South that season. We only went down because the Football

League were re-organising the divisions. All the teams in the lower half were relegated into a new Fourth Division. Totally beyond my control.'

'Those are definitely mitigating circumstances. Were there others too?'

'Of course. Too many to list. Come with me, I'll show you.'

McBain went to the shelf and took down two copies of Watford versus Brighton and Hove Albion on Saturday April 26th 1958 — the penultimate game of the season. He led Bill to the ancient turnstile.

*   *   *

At the Brighton match, Bill gazed around the stadium. The place looked tired and stale. The black awning over the players' tunnel was filthy; the duckboard over the dog track was falling apart; and The Rookery was just a shallow, featureless end without a stand. At first sight, Bill felt that a trip back to this season wouldn't be a relevant environment for making a point to Freddie Sargent about life as a Watford fan in 2016/17. The look of the place in 1958 didn't suggest that Watford had aspirations that the manager might be failing to fulfil.

On the other hand, there were some possible parallels, Bill thought. In 1958, Watford had been in the same division for 38 years — ever since they'd joined the Football League. They'd had no promotions, no relegations. In this respect, it was the same kind of existence to which Watford fans in 2016/17 now aspired in the Premier League — with no promotions and hopefully no relegations. Bill wondered if coming back to 1958 and seeing the staleness might make people think again about whether they really wanted to live with no ups or downs.

McBain interrupted Bill's thoughts. The Scotsman said: 'This match sealed our fate. We lost 1-0 and became founder members of Division Four.'

'And it definitely wasn't all your fault?' Bill asked.

'No way. For starters, some of the players threw this match. They took money so Brighton would win and be promoted. The News Of The World investigated and named our captain, Johnny Meadows. He admitted it.'

Bill and McBain watched as Johnny Meadows, cool as you like, led the Watford players, in their blue shirts with white v-necks, out of the tunnel to take the field.

'There's the culprit,' McBain said. 'But I was the one accused of taking Watford down.'

'To be fair, match-fixing was only a factor in this particular match. Was there anything else during the season that clearly wasn't your fault?'

'Oh aye. Definitely. The club sold my best player: Maurice Cook. He's in Hornet Heaven: he'll tell you it wasn't my fault. The board couldn't resist filling their boots with a record transfer fee: fifteen thousand pounds. Maurice was a forward who could score 31 goals a season and I wasn't given a replacement.'

'Well, there we are. Perfect. No-one could single you out as to blame. I'll bring Freddie Sargent here and he'll understand that you can never just blame the boss.'

McBain smiled. He was glad to help. More than this, though, he felt vindicated.

But then he said: 'Och, no.'

'What?' Bill said. 'What's the matter?'

McBain pointed in the opposite direction from where he'd been looking. He said: 'Er.. Look! Quick! Over there!'

Bill looked, but didn't see anything worth seeing. He turned back. Now he saw what McBain hadn't wanted him to see. It was the 1958 version of McBain coming out of the tunnel. The manager was slipping a hip flask back into his pocket and stumbling slightly on the dog track.

'McBain!' Bill exclaimed. 'And I thought it was bad that Walter Mazzarri smokes!'

'I was only having a wee nip. It took a lot more than that to render me incapable of doing my job, I can tell you.'

Bill didn't want to hear how much it had taken. He watched the real-world McBain get his trouser leg snagged on the wire fencing by the touchline. The gaffer hopped unsteadily as he tried to free himself.

'Look at you!' Bill said. 'Drunk in charge! You've given Freddie Sargent all the ammunition he'll need to destroy my argument!'

Bill turned on his heel. Going back to 1958 had proved pointless. He was furious. He marched back to the ancient turnstile muttering: 'That was a complete waste of time! And 100% down to McBain!'

* * *

Bill came out of the ancient turnstile onto Occupation Road. It was still overcast.

A large crowd had gathered below the banner that Freddie and Henry had hung from the roof of the stand.

Everyone was chanting 'Mazzarri Out! Mazzarri Out!'. Bill recognised Frank Gammon, a Watford fan who'd been a new arrival two years earlier. Frank was yelling furiously — as if the anger management issues he'd always had in the land of the living had resurfaced. Bill speculated that if Frank had brought one of his cats into Hornet Heaven, the old man would probably be about to punt it into the gardens behind the garages.

Bill glanced up at the roof and saw Freddie and Henry. They were conducting the chanting of the massed ranks below. Bill was left in no doubt that he was losing the argument — as comprehensively as Watford were likely to lose against Manchester City in their final game of the season in a few days' time. He badly needed a new idea to turn the situation around.

'Sir! Sir!' came a voice.

Bill turned and saw Derek.

'I've got your hut ready, sir. It's going to be a great way of calming Freddie Sargent down, sir. Shall I show you, sir? Shall I, sir?'

Bill wasn't terribly optimistic, but he let the boy lead him to the Bill Mainwood Programme Hut. First, Henry had rebuilt it as a confessional. Then it had been an IMAX cinema. Then an emergency clinic. Now

Derek said: 'Welcome to the Bill Mainwood Luxury Spa, sir. It's a place where anyone can lie back and have all their stresses disappear, sir. Perfect for Freddie Sargent — and the rest of the mob too, sir.'

'A spa, young man?'

'A flotation tank, specifically, sir. With litres and litres of relaxing warm water containing magnesium-rich Epsom salts.'

'But how on earth did you get the plumbing done?'

'There's a Watford fan up here called Pete Burkwood, sir. Died in 2015, sir. He was a plumbing and heating engineer. A lovely man, sir. Even though he had a few reservations about my design, sir, he agreed to help me for the good of the club.'

Bill stared at the Bill Mainwood Luxury Spa. From the outside, the red portacabin looked the same as it always had. Not very luxury.

Bill went to the door. He said: 'Well, I'm curious, young man. I'd like to see what you've done inside.'

'Wait a moment, sir. One of things Pete wasn't sure about was—'

'Don't spoil things by explaining, my boy. Much better if I go in and just use my eyes to appreciate the wonder of my refurbished hut.'

'No, sir! Don't! Stop!'

Bill opened the door. Hundreds of litres of relaxing warm water containing magnesium-rich Epsom salts poured out over him.

A few seconds later, Bill stood on Occupation Road, drenched from head to toe, with his glasses skewiff. He said: 'Judging from my stress levels right now, young man, I'm not convinced those Epsom salts actually work.'

Bill walked up Occupation Road, sopping wet. Derek followed him at a sheepish distance in the unusually grey light.

Derek said: 'There are some positives, sir. If you'd been wanting to witness a torrent of water, sir, it's saved you a trip back to the abandoned home game against Wigan in the Boothroyd Premier League season.'

Bill squelched up the slope past the chanting mob. Suddenly he heard Henry's voice from up on the roof. Henry was laughing.

'Ha! Look at Bill! Look at the absolute state of him!'

The mob turned and looked at Bill. The entire crowd started pointing and laughing.

Bill kept walking. He seethed. Through no fault of

his own, he'd become a whipping boy for Watford fans. It was as if he was walking a mile in Walter Mazzarri's shoes — though Walter's loafers would have felt a lot drier.

He was beginning to despair. He needed to make fans realise how blinkered they were whenever they singled out a fall guy for their frustration and disappointment — but he couldn't think how to do it.

Then suddenly — just before he got to the atrium — he knew exactly how he'd do it.

* * *

The next day, when he'd dried out, Bill went to see Roy in the IT department of Hornet Heaven.

Bill said: 'I want to show Freddie Sargent and the mob that it's unfair to single out one person as the cause of all their troubles. The fortunes of football clubs are never down to one man.'

'Are you sure about that, Bill?' Roy replied. 'What about—'

'It's definitely unfair.'

'I mean the one man bit. Don't forget—'

'Please, Roy. Just listen. This is urgent. I want to

know if what I've got in mind is possible.'

Roy listened as Bill outlined his new idea.

'I'd like to take everyone on a Magical History Tour, but there are far too many people. So I was wondering if you could download the main bits from the tour I've got in mind, edit them into highlights — or lowlights, in this case — and show them on one of the big video screens in the stadium.'

'Easy enough. What's the theme of the tour going to be?'

'I want people to see that it's unreasonable to scapegoat Walter Mazzarri. So the tour will be… "Scapegoats Through The Ages".'

'Nice. The boo boys will love that.'

'Exactly. But only at first. Then, when they see just how many players have been made victims over the years, they'll feel terrible and realise the error of their ways.'

Bill handed Roy a list of Watford Scapegoats Through The Ages. Then he headed off to spread the word about a special mystery screening that no-one should miss.

* * *

On the Sunday morning, on the day of Watford's match with Manchester City, Bill opened up the Players' Entrance to the stadium. The mob started to file through. They went down the steps, past the dressing rooms, through the tunnel, and out onto the pristine pitch. Bill followed.

On the touchline, Les Simmons — who was Watford's head groundsman for more than 30 years until the late 1990s — ran up to Bill. He said: 'Get these people off my pitch! They'll kick lumps out of it! Get them off!'

Bill remembered from his time working at the club how protective of the playing surface Les Simmons had always been. He reassured Les that no-one in Hornet Heaven could harm the real-world pitch. But Les still wasn't happy. The lean, weathered old man walked away, chuntering.

Before long, there were hundreds and hundreds of fans in the North West corner of the pitch, in front of the empty stands, looking up at the giant video screen. Behind them, up on the roof of the Sir Elton John stand, Freddie Sargent and Henry Grover had turned around and were sitting down to watch, with their legs dangling over the edge towards the pitch.

Bill stood in the middle of the crowd. Next to him was Frank Gammon. Frank was already in a terrible temper. At times like this he made Jose Holebas seem cherubic. Bill looked forward to seeing the enlightening effect that the video would have on Frank.

Soon, through a concealed microphone, Bill gave Roy in IT the signal to start the video — and the screen began to fill with historic Watford footage.

The show started with the Dave Bassett era. The crowd groaned. When Watford's right-back casually let a Luton player go past him, Frank Gammon shouted: 'Gary bloody Chivers! I couldn't stand him! Boooo!'

Other fans around Frank started booing too.

In the same match, a Watford forward mistimed a header, sending it straight up in the air. Frank yelled: 'Rubbish, Senior! Get off!'

There was more booing — louder this time.

Bill smiled. He reckoned his choice of scapegoats was proving perfect.

Soon there was footage from 1994. A Watford forward shot tamely wide. Frank shouted: 'Jamie Moralee was total crap! He couldn't hit Micky Quinn's arse with a banjo!'

Behind Bill, a group of fans giggled and booed.

Soon, the screen showed an away match at West Brom in April 2008. A forward was waiting to come on as a late substitute for Jobi McAnuff. Frank shouted: 'Steve Kabba! What a waste of space!'

Moments later, on screen, another forward appeared alongside Kabba, waiting to come on for John-Joe O'Toole. Frank shouted: 'Steve Kabba and Nathan Ellington! That has to be the worst double substitution in club history! For crying out loud! Boooo!'

Suddenly Bill noticed that the crowd around him seemed to be enjoying booing. As if the theme was "Pantomime Villains Through The Ages", not scapegoats.

Bill started to lose confidence in his plan. People were now in high spirits. There was definitely no sign that anyone was feeling bad about victimising Watford staff.

As the video showed footage from more recent seasons, Frank Gammon got more and more vociferous. The sight of Matthew Briggs made Frank blaspheme. The sight of Josh McEachran made Frank swear. The sight of Samba Diakite made Frank make up new terrible swearwords by combining existing terrible swearwords.

Other fans joined in with even more offensive abuse. Bill didn't like what he was hearing. He'd wanted his fellow fans to realise that scapegoating was wrong, but the video was whipping them into a frenzy. It was encouraging them to victimise Watford staff. His plan had completely backfired.

Now the screen showed Allan Nyom playing for Watford at the end of the previous season. The crowd spat insults at him. Then, when Nyom appeared in a West Brom shirt at The Hawthorns in December 2016, celebrating the Baggies' victory in front of the Watford away fans, everyone around Bill exploded with anger. They called Allan Nyom the worst word Bill had ever heard in his life or afterlife.

Bill didn't want things to get any worse. He shouted to Roy through his microphone: 'Stop! Stop the video!'

Immediately, the giant screen flickered and went black.

After a few seconds, Frank shouted: 'Boo! You can't stop it there! I want to see Mazzarri up there! I hate him more than any of that lot!'

A moment later, a chant started up: 'Mazzarri Out! Mazzarri Out!'

For the first time, Bill felt frightened. There was a new fervour to the chant, a new venom.

Bill didn't know what to do. His plan had resulted in the opposite of what he'd intended. The mob hadn't realised the error of its ways. Instead, it had become incensed. It looked as if things were about to get out of hand.

He watched Frank Gammon assemble a group of fans to form an angry mob. Frank didn't have any flaming torches, but he did go over to Les Simmons, the former head groundsman and ask: 'Les, mate. Where do they keep the pitchforks?'

Bill panicked and ran.

* * *

Bill sat in his office. He felt alone — one man alone, when the rest of the Watford family were thinking and feeling something completely different.

He also feared what the angry mob might be doing. His scapegoat video had stirred up a proper Hornets' Nest.

Suddenly he heard footsteps running towards the office — and a high-pitched voice.

'Sir! Sir!'

Bill looked up. Derek appeared in the doorway. The boy had a look of horror on his soft young face.

'Something terrible's happened, sir! Really terrible!'

Bill was fully aware, with hindsight, that his idea to show the video had been terrible. But judging from the look on the teenager's face, whatever had happened now was definitely worse. For few moments, Bill couldn't imagine what that would be.

Then Derek said: 'You need to come and see your hut, sir.'

* * *

Occupation Road seemed more clouded over than ever.

Bill stood and stared at his hut.

Derek said: 'The people who have done this are... combustible mutants, sir! This is... This is... Desecration, sir!'

Bill couldn't believe what he was seeing. There was anti-Walter graffiti all over the red walls of his portacabin. Foul language. Obscene drawings.

'Look at this, sir!' Derek squeaked. 'It says Walter

Mazzarri is a steaming pile of—'

'Don't say it!' Bill interrupted.

'And look at this drawing, sir! Walter's head doesn't look like his head at all, it looks more like someone's—'

'Nooooooo!'

Bill burst into helpless sobs. For years, the Bill Mainwood Programme Hut had stood on Occupation Road as one of the true icons of Watford Football Club. In the last few days, thanks to Henry, and despite Derek's recent silly idea, it had retaken pride of place and helped residents of Hornet Heaven come to terms with a difficult season. Now it stood daubed with obscenities. It had become a monument to hatred.

Bill lost control of his shoulders. They began to heave with grief.

Derek stepped forward in front of Bill. The teenager looked up at the old man. At first he wasn't sure what to do. Then he stood on tiptoe and wrapped his arms around Bill. Derek held on tightly as waves of anguish caused Bill's chest to convulse and shudder. The boy tried his hardest to stay strong. He tried not to cry.

But this wasn't just any distraught man. This was his boss, his stand-in uncle, the man he loved and respected most, the man in Hornet Heaven who always did the right thing.

It was all too much. A Hornet Heaven with a vandalised Bill Mainwood Programme Hut was not the Watford Derek knew and loved. He broke down and sobbed.

For several minutes, Derek and Bill clung to each other, crying inconsolably. From further up the slope they heard the sound of fans chanting for the sacking of the Head Coach, using the same foul language they'd used to deface the hut. As each minute passed, the light of Hornet Heaven seemed a little dimmer still.

But then the chanting stopped.

Bill and Derek released each other and turned to look up the slope. They saw a man walking towards them through the grey light. The fans who'd been chanting stepped out of his way. Some of them hung their heads. The man had said just three words to them: 'Watch your language'.

It wasn't just a man walking down Occupation Road.

It was The Great Man.

*   *   *

As always in Hornet Heaven, The Great Man was wearing a 1979 black Umbro tracksuit top with wide yellow and red panels down the front. Bill watched him arrive at the hut and inspect the graffiti. Then Bill felt The Great Man's arm around his shoulder and found himself being led gently up the slope.

They passed the silent crowd and crossed the sunless tarmac to a gate beside an old brick garage with mint green paint clinging to the wooden doors. The Great Man held the gate open for Bill and gestured him through. Bill stepped cautiously through the gate.

Suddenly, he wasn't anywhere near Occupation Road. He was in a park.

The Great Man led him across an expanse of grass. Ahead of them, surrounded by newly planted trees, was a brown wooden bench. The Great Man invited him to sit down.

Bill sat down. He noticed a plaque on the back of the bench. It said: IN LOVING MEMORY OF FRIEND GRAHAM TAYLOR. MUCH LOVED. ELTON.

The Great Man sat down and started talking to Bill with gentle words of sympathy, encouragement, and advice. Bill listened.

Bill loved the sound of The Great Man's voice. Maybe not as much as The Great Man had seemed to love it himself, sometimes, down on earth, but he definitely loved it. The mere sound of it always had a powerful effect on him. Its accent, tone and rhythms — instantly recognisable — somehow made him feel part of a community of people who believed in the same thing. The voice belonged to The Great Man — obviously — but also, in a way, it belonged to every single Watford fan.

As they sat on the bench, Bill found he wasn't concentrating on The Great Man's words. Instead, he felt awestruck. Here he was in the presence of the man who had transformed Watford Football Club. The man who'd built a focal point for a town. The man who had established values to play by and live by, for players and fans alike. Bill couldn't help marvelling at the way this one man had touched so many lives.

Suddenly Bill stopped marvelling. He replayed the thought he'd just had: 'One man'.

He replayed it again. '*One man* had touched so many lives.'

Bill covered his mouth with his hand. He'd been wrong. He'd been going around saying that the fortunes of a football club were never influenced by a single man. But next to him on the bench was proof that all the factors that caused football teams to disappoint *could* be overcome by one man — if that man was great enough.

Bill looked at The Great Man and fully recognised what the right man in charge could do for a football club.

He got up and thanked The Great Man — for everything in the past, and for helping him see things more clearly today. He now knew that Walter Mazzarri wasn't the right man in charge. The club should look for a leader who could lead and inspire — the way The Great Man had done, twice.

Bill Mainwood left the bench with a new conviction.

He wanted Walter Mazzarri out.

* * *

Bill arrived back into the dull light of Occupation Road through the gate. The crowd below Freddie's banner had started chanting again, but this time without the obscenities.

Bill joined the crowd. Now that he was standing with them, he thought they didn't look like 'combustible

177

mutants', or whatever Derek had called them. They looked like ordinary Watford fans who wanted better for their club — better than Walter Mazzarri seemed capable of delivering.

Bill joined in with the chanting. Not too loudly at first, but gradually increasing in volume as he realised how good it could feel. As he started to bellow, he properly understood why his scapegoat video idea had backfired. Ridding himself of all his pent-up angst felt fantastic. He wished he'd done it sooner.

He looked up to the roof. Freddie Sargent and Henry Grover were there, leading the chant. He jumped up and down and shouted 'Mazzarri Out' at them as loud as he could. Through the dim light, Freddie and Henry spotted him and shook their fists in delight. Bill felt elated to be part of the group. It had taken him a long time to accept what the rest of the Watford family were feeling, but he'd found a way in the end.

Soon, though, Bill felt a tug at his jacket. He looked down. He saw Derek.

'Sir! Sir!'

Bill stopped chanting and said: 'Sorry, young man. But I'm afraid I don't care if there's another crisis. I'm with everyone else now. I just want the burden of Walter

Mazzarri lifted.'

'No problem, sir. But I thought you ought to know that the Manchester City programme is in, sir.'

'Well, I can assure you I won't be rushing off to watch that. If Mazzarri's still in charge, we'll get horribly thrashed.'

Derek handed Bill the programme and said: 'But you need to look at page nine, sir. The Head Coach's programme notes, sir.'

'Oh. Really? Why?'

Bill flicked through the programme to page nine. Around him the crowd were still chanting: 'Mazzarri Out! Mazzarri Out!'

A few moments later Bill shouted at the top of his voice: 'Yes! Mazzarri is out!'

The crowd around him heard what he'd shouted.

They stopped chanting.

He waved the programme above his head and shouted again: 'Mazzarri is out!'

The crowd roared so loud it sounded like an aircraft taking off. Months of frustration and anger poured out of everyone.

Bill lifted his face to the sky in relief. It was only a piece of news about a member of staff, but it felt as good as The Great Escape had felt in 1991. All the misery and the pessimism was instantly over.

A few seconds later, as he stared upwards, Bill noticed something happening in the sky, high above Occupation Road. Overhead, the grey clouds were parting. The light was becoming brighter.

Within moments, the sun had broken through and was shining on Hornet Heaven again.

* * *

'Well, what do you think, old thing?' Henry asked. 'Do you like it?'

Bill stood in The Bill Mainwood Programme Hut and looked around. Henry had had the graffiti on the outside removed. He'd also had the inside of the hut refurbished.

On the walls were old match-day posters. In one of the corners there was a yellow black and red dartboard. In another corner there was a small bar with Watford beer towels and beer mats. And in the middle of the floor there were two deckchairs with yellow and black — not yellow and red — stripes.

Bill grinned. He said: 'The perfect place to chillax

after a trying season, Henry.'

'Exactly, Bill. I think we should call it The Bill Mainwood Man Cave.'

The two men lowered themselves into the deckchairs. They stretched out their legs and put their hands behind their heads. They sat and reflected on everything they'd been through recently with Freddie Sargent, Neil McBain, Mike Keen and Kelly.

After a while, Henry said: 'I tell you, old chap, I'm so glad 2016/17 is over.'

'I agree. We've been spanked 5-0 at home on the final day and avoided relegation by one league place, but now the slate has been wiped clean.'

'Absolutely, old thing. It'll be a fresh start. With a new manager to be appointed and lots of expensive new players coming in.'

'I quite liked the look of that Marco Silva who was in charge of Hull when we played them.'

'So did I. It would be splendid if the Mazzarri cloud turned out to have a Silva lining.'

Bill leaned forward in his deck chair.

'Now you're talking. We've got the owners, the stadium, and the resources. Marco Silva could be the one man we need to make everything come together.'

Henry frowned and said: 'The one man? Are you sure? Earlier you were saying—'

'I'm saying different now. One man could make the difference.'

Henry smiled at his old friend and said: 'I say, Bill. Isn't it great to be feeling ambitious again? When you think about it, we're already joint top of the table. We're level with Manchester City, Chelsea and all the other big teams on zero points for next season.'

Bill beamed at the thought. He'd developed a taste for chanting recently, so he shouted out: 'We are top of the league! I said, we are top of the league!'

Henry grinned and joined the chant: 'We are top of the league! I said, we are top of the league!'

They were ready for 2017/18.

THE END

10

THE TRIBUTE

EARTH SEASON 2017/18

One afternoon, in the summer of 2017, two long-deceased residents of Hornet Heaven were sitting in the empty Vicarage Road stadium. Bill Mainwood and Henry Grover were in the Upper Graham Taylor stand, gazing out over the magnificent green expanse below them.

Bill said: 'This re-laid pitch would grace the Champions League. You're a man with a keen eye for beauty, Henry. Would you say it's the greenest pitch in the entire history of the club?'

'To tell you the truth, old thing,' Henry replied, 'I've still got a soft spot for brown. In the 1960s, the club gave us mud in several fabulous shades. There was Moist Chestnut in March 1961. Congealing Coffee in January 1965. And most magnificently, during the championship-winning winter of 1968/69, Wet Beaver.'

'You mean you actually preferred soil to grass?'

'Very much so, Bill. I always felt that the raw earth added an exquisite depth and texture. And the thematic consistency with the stadium's surroundings was breathtaking.'

'Thematic consistency? What does that mean?'

'The pitch was basically a continuation of the allotments.'

'Oh. I see.'

'Whenever I arrived on a match day, I half-expected to see carrots growing in the Rookery goalmouth, and rows of purple-sprouting broccoli all the way up to the Vicarage Road end. The look just worked. Especially when the football was agricultural too. The old days were the best, Bill.'

'But those pitches must have been terribly difficult to play good football on. Can you imagine the skilled technicians of our current squad having to play on those surfaces?'

'My goodness. I'd love to see Roberto Pereyra's

thighs caked in mud.'

'To see if he can still play his defence-splitting passes?'

'No. Just Roberto Pereyra's thighs caked in mud.'

Bill frowned. He couldn't quite tell if Henry — the man who founded Watford Rovers in 1881 — was joking or not. He decided not to enquire, and moved the conversation on.

He said: 'You're right to value the past, though, Henry. The new owners may well have made this stadium truly magnificent, but we must never forget the people who built this club from the ground up — the giants on whose shoulders Gino Pozzo is standing.'

'Quite, old thing. Absolute giants,' Henry agreed. Then he hesitated. He asked: 'Er, were you, um, referring to me there, by the way?'

'To be honest, Henry, I was actually thinking of someone else. Sorry.'

'No, that's fine, Bill. That's fine. I guess I have to accept my true place in the Watford pantheon. In which case…'

Henry threw his arms wide towards the Vicarage Road and Rookery stands and shouted: '…praise be to Jack Petchey!'

'Jack Petchey? The East End taxi tycoon? He's not in the pantheon! He may well have built two new stands, but he left the soul of the club structurally unsound.'

'Ah. Actually, I was joking there, Bill. Sarcastically making the point that my own contribution is less visible than—'

'If you want to praise someone who genuinely transformed this club for the better, then his name is on the front of this very stand.'

'Indeed. The Great Man. It's so sad that he passed away so young. And yet…'

'"And yet"? There's no "and yet" to the sadness of The Great Man's passing.'

'But it's just that… Well, I don't mean to be insensitive, old chap, but from the very first day he joined us up here, everyone has been going on and on non-stop about what he did for the club. People call him "Mr Watford". But he didn't come along until 96 years after I founded the club. Sometimes I think—'

'Well, you can't under-state what he did for us. They named a stand after him in his lifetime, and now — in the land of the living — they're creating a statue and holding memorial games. They've never done that for anyone else.'

'That's true. I suppose I just have to recognise that my own role was never—'

'In fact, Henry, we should be doing exactly the same in Hornet Heaven. We should be establishing a lasting commemoration of The Great Man's achievements. Now there's a project for you!'

'But he's with us up here forever, old thing. He's his own lasting commemoration of his achievements.'

'The Great Man deserves more. In fact, Henry, as "The Father Of The Club", you should definitely be organising some kind of tribute to "The Most Important Person In The Entire History Of The Club".'

Henry winced at the difference between the two titles. He didn't think Bill had meant it as a withering put-down. Maybe his own inconsequence was simply the truth.

'There's no two ways about it,' Bill said. 'It's your duty to honour The Great Man. You need to come up with something really very special.'

Henry didn't feel he could argue with what Bill was saying. But he can't have looked very enthusiastic about the prospect because Bill said: 'Don't worry. It shouldn't be too difficult. I'll help you come up with something… I know, I'll take you on one of my "Magical History

Tours" — to The Great Man's greatest games. It'll inspire us. Ooh. In fact I've just had my first idea already.'

Bill stood up and said: 'We can't let The Great Man down. Come on, we're going on a Magical History Tour!'

*   *   *

Henry looked up the enormous floodlight pylon above them and said: 'Are you sure climbing up this thing is a good idea, old chap?'

'No, I'm not,' Bill replied. 'Which is exactly why we're going to give it a go.'

The two men had fetched programmes from the atrium and taken them through the ancient turnstile to go and watch a game from the original Graham Taylor era. They were in the south west corner — known in those days as 'The Bend'. The stadium looked very different. On their right was the tall shed of the old Rookery. On their left was the yellow Shrodells Stand.

They started to climb the huge floodlight pylon in the back corner. A few minutes later, after much puffing and blowing, 92-year-old Bill and 83-year-old Henry had scaled the vertical metal ladder and were clinging tightly to the steel struts of the pylon just below the lightbulbs.

Bill gazed across the stadium and said: 'What a view, Henry! This is definitely a good idea. You know, you really should open your eyes and take a look.'

Henry groaned: 'I wish I could. I didn't know I suffered from vertigo. Now I realise how Ross Jenkins must feel every day of his life.'

Z-Cars started up over the tannoy, and the Watford players came out. At the far end, the Vicarage Road terrace produced an explosion of confetti that descended slowly, shimmering, in the evening sky.

Bill grinned. May 4th 1982 was truly one of the greatest Vicarage Road nights ever. A win would put Watford in the top division of English football for the first time in history.

As Watford, in yellow and red, and Wrexham, in light blue and dark blue, lined up for kick-off, Bill explained his initial idea for a tribute to The Great Man.

'Watching from up the pylon here would be part of a special Magical History Tour to the most evocative games of The Great Man's time at the club. It would be called 'Great Nights Under The Lights'. The gimmick is that you'd be literally under the lights yourself as you watch. What do you think, Henry? Is it a good angle?'

Henry groaned: 'I'd say it's about 45 degrees too steep.'

'No, I mean the angle I've taken on our tribute to The Great Man: the special night games. I mean, what a sight this is! The bright lights against the black skies. The shining faces in the crowd. The kit gleaming yellow.'

Bill was surprised that Henry — Hornet Heaven's greatest aesthete — didn't seem at all enthusiastic about the vista below them. But when he turned and looked, Bill saw that Henry's eyes were still shut tight. Tighter than Wrexham fans' eyes would be in a few moments' time when Watford's Jan Lohman started flying into tackles

Bill tried a different tack. He said: 'And think of the games themselves, Henry. Here on this pitch. Beating Stoke after extra time in the League Cup in 1979. Winning promotion against Hull on that balmy night four months later. The 7-1 over Southampton. The 4-1 over European Champions Nottingham Forest eight weeks after that. Then tonight. Then, of course, Kaiserslautern!'

Bill checked to see if Henry was looking inspired.

But Henry wasn't. Henry was looking as if he might vomit.

'Oh dear,' Bill said. 'I do hope you develop a head for heights quickly — just like the club did under The Great Man. You see, we'd definitely want you accompanying people during the 'Great Nights Under The Lights' tour. It's important that the Founder is seen to be honouring the man who made the biggest contribution to the club in history.'

Henry groaned again, and spent the game with his eyes closed. He was pretty sure it was the vertigo making him feel sick, but there was another possible cause. Whenever people praised Graham Taylor's contribution to the club, Henry found himself feeling anxious inside. He had been the club's originator in 1881 — but it seemed he was no longer the most influential person in Hornet Heaven. He feared people would be starting to think he was a fraud. They'd think he was clinging onto his position as desperately as he was clinging onto this pylon. The last thing Henry wanted was to linger in a role where he'd lost respect. He didn't want to become a Walter Mazzarri.

He'd definitely never felt entirely at ease with the

title of 'Father Of The Club'. During his lifetime on earth, no-one had properly traced the formation of Watford Football Club back to Watford Rovers and Henry William Grover. Henry had seen out his life in the town without anyone acknowledging his original role. It had been a surprise to find himself venerated as the club's founder when he passed over to Hornet Heaven in March 1949.

In the Wrexham game beneath him, in the last minute, Ross Jenkins scored his second to secure Watford a 2-0 win. Twenty thousand Watford fans sent an ecstatic shout into the night sky. Soon they started chanting: 'One Graham Taylor! There's only one Graham Taylor!'.

Bill couldn't stop himself joining in, but Henry just clung to the pylon. He marvelled how fans had been singing the Great Man's name in 1982 and were still singing it 35 years later in 2017. But no-one — he reflected — had ever chanted the name of Henry Grover. Not once in 136 years. He reached the conclusion that this made his position as Father Of The Club completely untenable. He was, put simply, insignificant.

A few moments later, he opened his eyes to watch Watford seal promotion to the top flight for the first time. Steve Sherwood took a goal kick at the Rookery End down to Henry's right. The referee, in the centre circle, blew the final whistle and jumped to catch the ball, but missed it. All the players ran for cover as spectators swarmed onto the pitch from every direction. Luther Blissett, in the number eight shirt, sprinted towards the tunnel, dodging left and right to avoid colliding with the fastest-arriving fans; then Luther disappeared into a tide of delirious yellow.

It was a pinnacle moment in Watford's history at the time. A night of glory, and a night of widespread amazement at how high up the league ladder a small Hertfordshire club had climbed. But now Henry Grover, The Father Of The Club, watching from up above in 2017, was climbing *down* the pylon's metal ladder.

Bill called out: 'Henry! What's wrong?'

Henry didn't answer. He continued his despondent descent. The crowd on the pitch were chanting in praise of a man who'd led the club to the top echelon of English football. In comparison, all Henry had ever done was get permission for a group of pals to play in Cassiobury Park in 1881, and bring a football along.

In his head, Henry began to compose a letter of resignation.

* * *

The next day, Henry sat out on the balcony of the Gallery restaurant in the south west corner of the 2017 stadium. He hadn't got very far with composing his resignation letter. He'd got stuck on the very first line because he wasn't sure to whom he should be addressing the letter. Should he write "Dear Father Of The Club" or "Dear Me"? He was inclining towards the latter, if only because the phrase "Dear me, dear me" kept running through his mind whenever he contemplated his situation.

Now Henry heard the door onto the balcony opening. He turned and saw Bill. This time, Bill was with his young assistant from the programme office — Derek Garston.

Derek called out: 'Mr Grover, sir! Mr Grover, sir!'

The blue eyes of the soft-faced 13-year-old who'd died tragically young in 1921 were sparkling with excitement. He said: 'I've had a brilliant idea for what the Hornet Heaven tribute to The Great Man should be, Mr Grover, sir.'

Henry blanked Derek. He turned back to the pitch.

Everyone was continuing to be obsessed with The Great Man's greatness. It was starting to get his hackles up.

Bill and Derek sat down either side of Henry.

Bill said: 'Derek's idea is to hold a Graham Taylor Match Day, Henry — like they're doing in the land of the living.'

Henry replied: 'Well, there's nothing brilliant about that as an idea.'

'Ah, but its brilliance lies in what it would symbolise, Henry. You see, Derek's idea is to stage a game between two teams of Hornet Heaven residents, down there on the real-world pitch, playing for the Hornet Heaven Graham Taylor Trophy. One team would be made up of players from the early days of Watford Rovers, and the other team would be made up of Watford players from more recent eras.'

'But that wouldn't be a fair contest,' Henry said. 'The team of more recent players would obviously win. They played at a much higher level.'

'Exactly, Henry. Thereby symbolising the club's transformation over the years. And who oversaw the biggest transformation at Watford? The Great Man. It would be a wonderful acknowledgement of what he did for us.'

'Wait. The players from the Taylor years aren't in Hornet Heaven yet — thank goodness. So the Watford team in this proposed match of yours would have to come from earlier eras. Why does The Great Man deserve credit for Cliff Holton being an amazing player? What the match actually symbolises is that the club advanced dramatically *before* The Great Man arrived.'

At this point, young Derek gleefully grabbed Henry's sleeve. He said: 'But that's the complete and utter genius of my idea, Mr Grover, sir. We'd make The Great Man the manager of the obviously better team, Mr Grover, sir! So all the credit would go to him!'

'Ah. Right,' Henry said. 'I see that how that works. But… Hang on. Who would be the mug who ends up managing the obviously worse team?'

Derek's eyes sparkled more than ever. He said: 'You, of course, Mr Grover, sir! You founded the obviously worse team, so you have to manage them!'

Henry sat back in his seat. He sharply prised Derek's small fingers from his sleeve. He pushed the boy's hand away. It was one thing to have arrived by himself at the sense that he was a trivial footnote in the club's history. It would be quite another to be publicly humiliated for his irrelevance. He said: 'No. No, no, no...'

But as he was saying it, some of the old Henry Grover fighting spirit began bubbling up inside him. It was the same fighting spirit that had seen him keep the club going during its difficult initial years; the same fighting spirit with which he'd marshalled the Watford Rovers defence in the rumbustious early days of association football. Suddenly he felt up for the challenge. Managing a Watford Rovers team to beat The Great Man's team was a chance to show everyone — including himself — that he was, after all, a man of influence at Watford Football Club in 2017.

He finished his sentence: 'No, no, no... no problem.'

Then he looked Bill Mainwood firmly in the eye and said: 'Bring it on!'

* * *

Two evenings later, the floodlights were on at Vicarage Road, and Henry Grover was sitting in the home dug-out.

Henry had always had a bit of a thing about the dug-out seats. Not just for their striking contours —

which, for Stefano Okaka, he'd noticed last season, were really quite figure-hugging — but also for the bold statement of the Watford colour-scheme that Henry strongly preferred. Bill Mainwood, who preferred yellow and black, had once suggested they looked like horribly garish car seats — possibly from a clown car. In reply, Henry had sniffed that they were more likely seats from the first class section of the metaphorical private jet in which Watford had soared into the Premier League under Gino Pozzo.

Henry looked out onto the floodlit arena. The "Hornet Heaven Graham Taylor Tribute Match" was about to kick off, as a night game, on the pristine Vicarage Road turf. The stands on all four sides of the stadium were packed with Hornet Heaven residents. There wasn't a spare seat. The place was absolutely rocking. It was already a special Vicarage Road night.

Henry got to his feet. He knew the match was all about The Great Man, but he wanted to make his own mark as well. It was time for Henry Grover, Father Of The Club and Manager For The Day, to inspire his underdog team. He summoned the Watford Rovers players from their warm-up on the glorious surface.

'OK, team. Gather round!'

Henry glanced at the other technical area — where The Great Man himself was already giving a pep-talk to his team of Watford legends. The Great Man, as always in Hornet Heaven, was wearing a black 1979 tracksuit top with wide yellow and red vertical panels. His team had borrowed replica shirts from Watford fans in Hornet Heaven. Tommy Barnett was wearing the classic 1984/85 shirt; Cliff Holton was in the stripey affair from 2015/16. They looked like they meant business — and The Great Man was in full flow. Henry knew he'd have to pull off something extraordinary to defeat The Most Important Person In The History Of The Club.

Henry turned back and inspected his own men as they assembled on the touchline. In contrast to their opponents, they didn't look at all ready for a sporting contest. With no Watford Rovers replica shirts available, his team were wearing the clothes they'd been buried in: dark suits and everyday boots. Some were wearing hats.

Henry told himself, for possibly the first time in his afterlife, that aesthetics didn't matter. He cleared his throat and said above the noise of the crowd: 'Now listen to me, gentlemen.'

A voice immediately replied: 'Why should we?'

Henry groaned silently. He didn't need this. The

voice belonged to Freddie Sargent, the cantankerous Watford Rovers forward who had spent his life and afterlife protesting against things he didn't like — from professionalism in the late nineteenth century to Walter Mazzarri in 2017.

But Henry didn't back down. He said firmly: 'You have to listen to me, Freddie, because I'm the manager.'

'Watford Rovers never had a manager.'

'Well, we've got one today. Now, as I was about to say—'

'Watford Rovers won the Herts Senior Cup three times without a manager. We'll play far better without one. Especially if it's a total novice like you. Being The Father Of The Club doesn't qualify you for anything. I'm not playing under you.'

Henry could feel his self-esteem shrinking again. He acted swiftly and said: 'Right, Freddie. You're dropped.'

'You can't drop me. I was the club's best player bar none.'

'I'm in charge, Freddie, and I'm not standing for your nonsense. We'll play with ten men. Go back to the dressing room.'

As Freddie stormed off down the tunnel, Henry

wondered if he was doing the right thing. He glanced across at The Great Man. The Great Man nodded approvingly.

Henry felt a huge surge of confidence. He'd impressed The Great Man! Suddenly Henry felt he was a world-beater — exactly the way Luther Blissett felt from the very first day Graham Taylor walked through the doors of Vicarage Road.

Henry turned back to his team and started to improvise his first-ever team-talk.

'Right then, Rovers. You can tell I'm not messing around today. You're going to win me this game. Without Freddie.'

Henry noticed several players nodding — notably Alf and Alec Sargent. He was relieved to see that the remaining two Sargent siblings were sticking with him rather than siding with Freddie. The Coles brothers nodded too — Walter and Percy. Henry remembered how Watford Rovers had been a true band of brothers in the early days. He felt a surge of pride in his men.

He continued: 'I've picked you because you were this club's very first heroes. You led the way for everything that followed.'

The Sargent and Coles brothers shook their fists and

shouted.

'And let's be clear about something else,' Henry said. 'Your opponents today are nothing more than Johnny-come-latelies. None of them have your pioneering courage, your fight.'

The whole team roared.

Henry finished by shouting: 'Now, get out there and bring home the Hornet Heaven Graham Taylor Trophy!'

With another roar, the Watford Rovers team turned and ran to their positions in the Rookery half.

Henry sat down in the fancy yellow and red seats in the dug-out as Bill Mainwood, the referee for the evening, blew the whistle to start the match. Henry clenched his fists. He genuinely believed they could win this.

* * *

Twenty minutes later, Henry cut a frustrated figure on the edge of his technical area. His ten-man side were already three goals down.

He couldn't blame his team's average age of around 74, because The Great Man's team had the same average. But he was desperately disappointed by the

Watford Rovers performance. It reminded him of the display of 'walking football' that had been staged at Vicarage Road during the previous season. Not the one put on by middle-aged men at half-time, but the far less lively display of walking football by Walter Mazzarri's team at home to Stoke City.

Cliff Holton had opened the scoring for Watford with a 40-yard pile-driver into the Rookery goal, after a knock-down from Dennis Uphill. The crowd had gone crazy at what they saw as a re-creation of pretty much every single one of his 48 goals in 1959/60, as they remembered them.

Then the home-grown star of the years between the wars, Tommy 'Boy' Barnett, had jinked into the box and been brought down. In the land of the living, Tommy had never been entrusted with a penalty before — despite scoring 163 career goals for the club. Now he'd finally taken his first ever penalty for Watford. He'd despatched it as if he'd been doing it since 1928.

The next goal had come from Charlie White, Watford's 6th highest scorer of all time with 81 league goals. Charlie had mostly played during the Cassio Road years, but had scored the last of his goals here at Vicarage Road during the club's very first season at the new stadium in 1922/23. Ninety-five years later, his low drive put The Great Man's team three goals ahead.

Henry stared down at the immaculate turf at his feet. It looked like his chance to make a proper mark at the club — by beating The Great Man — had gone.

When he looked up, he saw a yellow-shirted Larry McGettigan, the winger from Watford's particularly useless seasons in the early 1970s, run past the suited and booted Alec Sargent. At the age of 41, McGettigan was younger and fitter than anyone else on the pitch. Henry knew it was all relative, but — for the first time ever at Vicarage Road — Larry McGettigan didn't look completely hopeless as he rounded the Rovers goalkeeper and made it 4-0.

The capacity crowd roared. Henry hadn't anticipated they'd be so strongly in favour of The Great Man's Watford side. He returned to his seat. He didn't feel like a world-beater any more. After Rovers gave the ball away from the kick-off and conceded a fifth, Henry moaned to himself: 'Dear me.'

Then he continued mentally composing the rest of his resignation letter.

Five minutes before half-time, Henry saw Walter Coles, one of Rovers' five forwards, sit down on the turf clutching his calf. Henry had been at a low ebb, but this suddenly incensed him. How could anyone in Hornet Heaven get a muscle injury? They were ghosts. They were plasma, or something, not flesh and blood. Henry ran to the edge of his technical area and shouted: 'You don't get cramp in Hornet Heaven!'

In the adjoining technical area, The Great Man recognised the reference and grinned.

This time, Henry didn't feel inspired by The Great Man's approval. He took the grin the wrong way. It looked to him like a smile of superiority. He scowled. A manager who hadn't turned up until 1977 was consigning the founder of the club to eternal anonymity. It wasn't right.

Henry's jaw tightened. His defeatism evaporated. He decided he had to do something to get his ten men back in the game.

Very quickly, he realised what was necessary. He wasn't sure how he'd do it, or what it would cost him, but it was the only answer.

He went down the tunnel to get Freddie Sargent back on the pitch for Watford Rovers.

* * *

Henry marched into the home dressing room. He came to a sudden halt. He hadn't been here before and he was immediately taken with the place. He stood and admired the slick black lockers, finished off with a monochrome club badge. He marvelled at the curvature of the black and red padded seats. He'd never seen anything like it. When he'd brought his ball along to Cassiobury Park for the very first Watford Rovers kick-around in 1881, he'd had to get changed behind a tree.

In the far corner, Henry saw Freddie Sargent in a red seat in front of a locker, leaning forward disconsolately. Henry galvanised himself. He knew Freddie was the only person who could turn things round on the pitch for Watford Rovers. He had to persuade Freddie to get out there and do the business.

He walked past the tea-cups that had been set out for half-time and said: 'Right, Freddie. I'm giving you a chance to reprieve yourself.'

Freddie didn't look up. He kept his head bowed and said: 'Not interested.'

'Come off it, Freddie, I don't believe that for one moment. A man like you must want to go out there and prove yourself.'

Freddie didn't answer.

Henry stood in front of Freddie and said: 'Think about it, Freddie. I'm giving you the chance to play for Watford Rovers. Something you haven't done for more than a century.'

Freddie still didn't look up. He said: 'Herts County Cup Semi-final, 3rd replay, against Watford St Mary's. 122 years, 3 months and 18 days ago.'

'There, you see. If you've been counting the days, Freddie, you really must take this chance to go out and represent the Rovers again.'

Freddie lifted his head. He said: 'Alright, then.'

Henry grinned. He'd persuaded his star player to play.

But then he stopped grinning. There was a look in Freddie's eye that Henry didn't like.

'I'll play,' Freddie said, 'but on one condition.'

Henry wasn't ready to back down. He said: 'Sorry, Freddie. I'm not going to stand down as manager. I'm afraid that's non-negotiable.'

'That's not the condition.'

Freddie stood up and said into Henry's face: 'You have to stand down as Father Of The Club. Right now.'

Freddie's demand hit Henry hard. His eyes

widened. Up to this point, the idea of giving up his role had been his and his alone. The idea had been that he would resign on his own terms — because he felt he should. But now someone else was demanding he quit. This was a whole new ball game.

Freddie added: 'You have to go out there, in front of everybody, as Father Of The Club, and sack yourself.'

Henry felt a tremble enter his hands. Now it entered his heart. He hadn't wanted things to reach this crisis point. His thoughts of resignation had been intended to pre-empt his falling out of favour — before he became unloved in Hornet Heaven; unloved for eternity. He looked into Freddie's eyes. There was no love whatsoever.

Henry's eyes welled up. The room receded as a blur. Over the years, there had been scenes of great joy in the Watford home dressing room. Henry had seen photos in programmes. Bottles of champagne foaming. Players splashing in the communal bath. John Barnes wearing ghastly white briefs. These had been moments of exuberant celebration. This moment, right now, was definitely not one of those.

Henry felt for a seat and sat down. He was feeling dazed. But not too dazed to notice, through the teardrops, that he was in a black seat. He shifted into a red one. Even when all felt lost, expressing the correct colour preference still mattered to him.

He heard Freddie say: 'Look at you, Grover. You're a loser. A nothing. Do you know how you're remembered in the land of the living? You get a mention on a neglected family gravestone in Vicarage Road Cemetery. A new arrival told me about it. Right at the bottom it says: "Also, Henry William Grover, passed away March 22nd 1949, aged 83." Nothing else. You're just a post-script on a forgotten headstone.'

Henry had never heard this before. He replied weakly: 'Is that all? "Also, Henry William Grover"?'

'You're an also-ran,' Freddie growled. 'That's all you're worth out there in the real world.'

Henry stared across the dressing room. His eyes cleared a little when tears finally ran down his cheeks. It was almost as if this news about his grave was helping him see his whole situation more clearly than ever.

He stood up, unsteadily and said with a faltering voice: 'Thank you for telling me, Freddie. I'll… I'll go and tell everyone I'm not… not worthy to be the Father of this club.'

Head bowed, Henry made his way back to the door.

A few steps later, he sensed something ahead of him just beyond the doorway. He looked up.

In the tunnel, players in yellow shirts were filing past on their way to the other dressing room. In front of them stood a man in a black 1979 track suit top — The Great Man. The Great Man was frowning. He didn't like what he'd just witnessed.

Henry stopped. He swallowed. He stared at The Great Man. Something came over him. Like dozens of people before him, he wanted to please The Great Man.

The Great Man raised his right hand and pointed at something to the side of Henry.

Henry turned and looked. He saw the set of half-time tea cups. He thought he knew what The Great Man meant but, when he turned back to check, The Great Man had gone.

Henry felt the same surge of confidence he'd felt earlier. If The Great Man had told him to do it, it was what he had to do. Without a moment's hesitation he grabbed a tea cup. He launched it. It smashed against the black locker behind Freddie's head.

Henry marched back across the floor and said firmly: 'Right. I'm the Father Of The Club, Freddie Sargent, and that isn't going to change. It's you that needs to change.'

Freddie, startled, toppled back down into his seat.

Henry stood over him and said: 'This football club has values. It always has done. Ever since day one in Cassiobury Park.'

Henry heard the sound of boots on the floor of the dressing room behind him. But he didn't stop speaking.

'This club stands for respect for others. Hard work. Team work. Generosity of spirit. You've shown none of those today.'

Henry heard voices behind him. Murmurs of agreement. He continued: 'You need to change, Freddie Sargent. If you can't live and breathe this club's values, your soul won't truly belong in Hornet Heaven.'

Henry felt an arm around his left shoulder. He felt another around his right shoulder. He looked in both directions and saw that his players had formed a tight line either side of him, standing tall, standing strong. Standing with The Father Of The Club.

Freddie Sargent looked up and down the line. He saw nothing but solidarity.

He nodded. He got to his feet. He said: 'Right. How many do you need me to score?'

The Watford Rovers players, to a man, roared, and

headed straight back out of the dressing room to warm up for the second half.

* * *

The second half of the Hornet Heaven Graham Taylor Tribute Match was extraordinary. It was definitely far more exciting than anything Watford fans had seen so far in 2017 while Walter Mazzarri was in charge.

Throughout the half, Henry stood on the edge of his technical area and watched his hopes of becoming a Watford hero — by managing an inferior team to victory over The Great Man — dramatically resuscitated.

First he saw Freddie Sargent dispossess Larry McGettigan, shrug off a challenge from Arthur Woodward, and fire past Skilly Williams into the roof of the Rookery End net for Rovers's first goal. Henry clenched his fists and muttered: 'That's more like it.'

Then he saw Freddie Sargent shoulder-charge The Big Fella to win the ball, nutmeg Tommy Barnett, and chip Skilly Williams from thirty yards. Henry punched the air and shouted: 'Get in, you beauty!'

Then Freddie left Taffy Davies, Maurice Cook and George Catleugh in his wake on a mazy dribble that ended with him rounding Watford's podgy keeper for a hat-trick. Henry sang deliriously: 'Have my baby, Freddie Sargent!'

After that, Freddie created goals for others. The crowd knew they were seeing something special. They began cheering every Watford Rovers touch. Henry was overjoyed. Freddie Sargent was showing all the values Henry had asked for. Respect for others. Hard work. Team work. Generosity of spirit.

With a minute to go, Watford Rovers levelled the scores at 7-7. The crowd's roar was like a crack of thunder. Henry sprinted down the touchline towards the Rookery End and did a knee-slide all the way to the corner flag, screaming with joy.

When he got back, still elated, he saw his team win the ball back from the kick-off and give it to Freddie Sargent. Henry waved his team forward manically. He was just one goal away from beating The Great Man. One goal away from historic relevance.

Henry watched as Freddie played a one-two with his brother Alec. Further up the pitch Freddie played another one-two — with his brother Alf. Freddie moved into the penalty box. He was drawing back his right foot to shoot when he was clattered from behind by George

Catleugh. Henry screamed: 'Penalty! Penalty!'

Bill Mainwood pointed to the spot.

Henry punched the air. The crowd roared. Henry turned to face the fans in the Sir Elton John Stand and did a little dance in his technical area.

But when Henry turned back to face the pitch, suddenly he didn't feel like dancing any more. Freddie Sargent was limping off the pitch with the ball in his hands.

Freddie said: 'I can't go on, Henry.'

'What? How can you be injured? It's not possible.'

Henry began to fret. Freddie was the only Watford Rovers player he fancied to score from the spot. He wasn't totally sure the others would know what to do. For the first ten years of the club's existence, the penalty kick hadn't been invented.

Henry surveyed the pitch, trying to work out who should take the penalty. Percy Coles saw Henry looking at him. He started clutching his hamstring and shaking his head. Mystery injuries started appearing all over the pitch. Alec Sargent suddenly started rubbing his knee. Alf Sargent fell to the turf in apparent agony, both hands around his ankle.

Freddie said: 'There's nothing for it. You'll have to

come on as substitute and take the penalty yourself, Henry.'

'Me? But I haven't played since our 3-2 win over Uxbridge Caxtonians in the Hennessey Cup 2nd round in December 1889.'

'We need you, Henry.'

'But… But I was always terrible. I was only in the team because I brought along the ball.'

'That's not true.'

'It is. I didn't play in the first half earlier — when we had ten men — because my presence would have made it seem more like nine men, or eight. Or seven.'

Freddie pressed the ball into Henry's hands and said: 'Get on there and score the winning goal.'

Henry stood on the touchline, holding the ball, terrified. The crowd realised what was going on. From all four sides of the stadium, they yelled encouragement. Henry stepped tentatively onto the pitch and made his way slowly and nervously towards the Rookery End goal.

Henry tried to visualise what he would do. The penalty kick may not have been invented until after he'd hung up his football boots, but over the years he'd seen plenty of Watford players succeed in this very goal. For a moment, he wondered whether to try and emulate the finesse of Keith Eddy. In the end he decided to go for the brute force of Troy Deeney against Manchester United the previous season.

Henry arrived at the penalty spot. He placed the ball and looked up. The portly figure of Skilly Williams in front of him seemed to fill the entire goal. Henry took five paces back. The noise of the crowd willing him to score was almost deafening. He tried to shut it out.

He polished the toe of his right boot on the left calf of his suit trousers.

He started his run-up.

He struck the ball.

The back of the net ballooned.

8-7 to Watford Rovers.

What happened next was all a bit of a blur for Henry — maybe because of the tears in his eyes; maybe because he just couldn't process the joy. He was aware of Freddie Sargent sprinting onto the pitch to celebrate with his team-mates, none of them with any sign of injury after all. He was aware of ecstatic fans swarming down from the stands and onto the pitch. He was aware of being lifted above the crowd's heads and finding himself crowd-surfing back towards the dug-outs. All against a backdrop of astonishing noise.

He'd never seen anything like it, heard anything like it, or felt anything like it in the 136 year existence of the club.

* * *

After the match, there was a presentation of the trophy. There were still thousands of fans on the pitch, but they made space for Bill Mainwood to perform the ceremony on the touchline in front of the Sir Elton John Stand. Bill stood with the two managers — Henry and The Great Man — either side of him.

As the three men waited for the crowd to quieten down, Henry noticed The Great Man was having a discreet word in Bill's ear. Bill was nodding.

Soon, Bill addressed everyone in Hornet Heaven. Holding the silver cup, he said: 'Ladies and gentlemen, girls and boys. It's time for the presentation of the Graham Taylor Trophy.'

The crowd applauded.

Bill continued: 'Except that — actually — it isn't.'

Henry was still finding things a bit blurry, but this got his attention. He didn't understand.

Bill explained to the crowd: 'What I mean is, there's been a bit of a last-minute change. This game wasn't for the Graham Taylor Trophy after all.'

Henry frowned. He absolutely didn't understand.

'You see,' Bill said, 'it's been decided to rename the trophy. In honour of a man who hasn't been honoured enough over the years.'

Now Henry knew what was coming. He felt a tremble entering his hands and heart again. But a good one this time. He saw Bill glance at The Great Man, and The Great Man nod.

Bill announced: 'Today's match was, in retrospect, the inaugural tribute match to the "Original Mr Watford". It was the first annual Henry Grover Match Day, playing for the Henry Grover Trophy."

The thousands of Hornet Heaven residents on the pitch and in the stands roared their approval. Henry welled up. He whispered to himself 'Dear me, dear me'. This time, it wasn't the start of a letter.

As the crowd cheered, Bill passed Henry the cup. Henry took it and looked out over the sea of happy Hornet Heaven faces. He held it aloft.

The crowd cheered even louder. At first it was just an ear-splitting mess of noise. But slowly it took shape.

It coalesced. It became a single, forceful, exuberant chant. They sang: 'One Henry Grover! There's only one Henry Grover!'

* * *

An hour later, Henry hadn't left the scene of the great turnaround. He was sitting in the home dug-out — relaxing with his hands behind his head and his legs stretched out either side of the Henry Grover Trophy on the ground in front of him. Bill Mainwood was with him.

Henry said: 'You know, old thing, today has been marvellous. It was just what I needed.'

Bill replied: 'Well, I feel a bit bad for not realising you'd been having so many doubts about your position as Father Of The Club, Henry. I was a proper silly billy.'

'Don't blame yourself, old chap. Everyone knows from the Bassett and Vialli managerial disasters that The Great Man was a difficult act to follow, but it wouldn't have occurred to anyone that he's also a difficult act to precede.'

Henry felt it was time to move on. He got to his feet and picked up the trophy. Bill got up too. They turned and started walking slowly towards the tunnel.

'So you're feeling in a better place now?' Bill asked.

'Definitely,' Henry replied. 'And I know my place now. The Great Man is definitely The Most Important Person In The Entire History Of The Club — there's no debate about that, whatever happened on the pitch today. He's also undoubtedly The Most Wonderful Human Being In The Entire History Of The Club: his generosity in suggesting that the trophy and matchday be renamed in my honour was remarkable yet typical. We're all in his shadow, Bill. I'm lucky that, once a year in Hornet Heaven, for eternity, my name will be just a little in the limelight.'

Bill nodded as they entered the tunnel. Henry summarised: 'I'm content with a passing mention. Just like on my gravestone.'

Bill didn't get the reference to the gravestone. He carried on walking down the tunnel. But Henry stopped for one last look back at the arena.

It was silent now. Henry gazed at the pitch as it lay waiting for the events of 2017/18 to unfold on its flawless expanse. He gazed at the yellow, red and black seats that were ready to welcome fans who would once again be experiencing moments that would become memories for the rest of their lives and afterlives. And finally he gazed at The Graham Taylor Stand on the far side — a permanent reminder, in concrete, of the man who would always be, for eternity, unarguably, the *real* "Mr Watford".

Henry smiled. He said quietly to himself "Also, Henry William Grover", and followed Bill down the tunnel.

THE END

11

THE PLASTIC

EARTH SEASON 2017/18

Freddie Sargent was a tetchy, petulant man. He was the Holebas of Hornet Heaven.

But today the moustachioed Watford Rovers forward from the 1880s and 1890s was no joyless José. It was the first day of the 2017/18 season and Watford had just scored a late equaliser at home to Liverpool. In the pandemonium in the Rookery End, Freddie had found himself hugging strangers. He'd even planted a big bristly kiss on someone's forehead.

Now he emerged from the ancient turnstile with one of those strangers. As they arrived on Occupation Road, Freddie said: 'I hope I didn't break any of your ribs, mate. I got a bit carried away. What a brilliant bundle.'

The stranger was a man in his late twenties. He had an expensive haircut and wore a dark pin-stripe suit with a salmon pink tie. He said: 'Yah — super, wasn't it? I tell you, good buddy, Watford being on a par with Liverpool makes me feel great.'

'Too right, mate,' Freddie agreed. 'But listen. I ain't seen you around before. Are you new in Hornet Heaven?'

'Pretty recent, good buddy. You may not have seen me, though, because I don't actually go to many games.'

'What?'

'Yah, I tend to pick and choose which I go to.'

'Pick and choose? No proper fan does that.'

'I do. I only watch us when we're playing the Big Clubs.'

'Hang about. You can't only support Watford in the big games. That makes you a… a Plastic Fan!'

'Nonsense, good buddy. It just makes me selective about the games I watch. It's the way I always was, back on earth. Just the high profile games.'

'You bloody Plastic! You disgust me. You shouldn't even be in Hornet Heaven. And to think I hugged you! Ugh! I feel physically sick!'

Hey, that's a tad harsh, good buddy. I've got every right—'

'No! You've got no rights at all! You're a Plastic, and I'm going to get you kicked out of Hornet Heaven!'

* * *

Freddie didn't wait. Straight after the Liverpool game, he went to see his old team-mate Henry Grover — the man who founded Watford Rovers in 1881. The Father Of The Club was in the Hornets Shop, admiring the new season's shirts.

'Mmmmm,' Henry sighed ecstatically. 'Ahhh. Oooooh. Ahhh.'

'Grover! What the hell are you doing?' Freddie barked.

'Mmmmm. Yellow and… red! '

Freddie grabbed Henry by the shoulder and yelled: 'Grover!'

'What? Ah. Hello, Freddie. I was just, er…. Yes. Well. I mean, this new kit really is quite gorgeous.'

'There's no time for any of that, Grover. We've got a serious problem.'

'Not with this new shirt, we haven't. It's Adidas.

Adidas, Freddie! I've been waiting decades to see three stripes on a Watford shirt. I'm afraid I simply can't contain my excitement.'

'Shut up and listen, Grover. This is important. There's a new arrival in Hornet Heaven who shouldn't be here.'

'What?'

'Good. Finally got your attention, have I?'

'Golly. Yes, you have. This chap isn't from up the road, is he? Not from the town that dare not speak its name? Don't tell me he's a... a... say the word for me, Freddie.'

'Scummer?'

'Ugh. Yes. Is he one of those?'

'No, he's not. He's nearly as bad, though. You'd better brace yourself for this, Grover... There's a plastic fan in Hornet Heaven.'

'Oh. Well, that's no big deal. We're all made of plastic in Hornet Heaven.'

'We're made of plasma, you idiot. Ghosts are made of plasma. A plastic fan is completely different. Not like us at all.'

'Oh. So, if he's plastic, what is he? A toy? Some kind of action figure? Does he have long arms and legs you can bend at weird angles — like Etienne Capoue does with his own arms and legs?

'No. A Plastic is a fake — someone who only turns up during the good times. Someone who wants in on the team's glory but isn't prepared to put in the hard yards. This one says he's only interested in the high profile games against the big clubs.'

'But what's wrong with that? We want more people at the big matches. It's what makes big matches big.'

'It's a matter of principle. Plastic fans want to bask in reflected glory. They don't pay their dues like real fans. Up here in Hornet Heaven, they should be made to go to every single game we've ever played against... oh, I don't know... Grimsby Town. Yeah. All 46 of the league games we've played against Grimsby. That's a lower division season's worth. That would definitely sort this bloke out.'

'But why are you so down on him? He does support the club. Surely that's what we want? This seems like a fuss about nothing.'

'This isn't nothing! He's a Plastic, Grover! As Father Of The Club, you need to do something!... Grover?'

'Mmmmm. Ahhh.'

'For crying out loud, Grover. You're not listening to me, are you?'

'Yellow and… red. Yellow and… red'

'Right. You haven't heard the last of this, Grover. You watch me. I'm going to do whatever it takes to get this bloke out of Hornet Heaven.'

* * *

Freddie stomped off to see Bill Mainwood, the Head Of Programmes in Hornet Heaven. Bill was in his office, just off the atrium, with his 13-year-old assistant Derek Garston.

'Something must have gone wrong,' Freddie said to Bill. 'I mean, how can a Plastic have got into Hornet Heaven?'

'The process is automatic,' Bill replied.' If you love the Horns, you just arrive here.'

'Do me a favour. Plastics don't love the Horns. I don't understand how he's got here.'

Derek took the chance to pipe up: 'Sir, I've always said there should be an entrance exam for Hornet Heaven. A basic knowledge test. Everyone should be able to name the team line-up from, say, the club's first recorded home win when Watford Rovers beat The Reverend David Patterson's XI 2-1 in October 1882, sir.'

'The team line-up from that, young man? Don't you think that's setting the bar quite high?'

'Not at all, sir.' Derek took a deep breath and recited: 'Wheeler, Horton, Capell, Grover, Valentine, Hurndall, Waterman, Horton, Smith, Christmas, Grace.'

Bill and Freddie stared at the boy.

'What, sir? Why are you looking at me like that, sir? Doesn't every Watford fan know that line-up?'

'Enough of the kid's nonsense,' Freddie said. 'The Plastic shouldn't be in Hornet Heaven. Watford fans up here love the Horns unconditionally. Not just when it suits them.'

'But perhaps he does love the club,' Bill replied, 'just in a different way from the rest of us. Not all Watford fans are exactly the same.'

'Rubbish. It's the glamour of Big Time football he's into. He won't be in love with Lloyd Doyley — like all proper Watford fans are. I tell you: this bloke's a wrong 'un.'

'Or perhaps it's such a deep-seated love that it hasn't quite realised itself yet in the usual way. The simple fact is, Freddie, that, if he's here, he must love Watford.'

'Well, in that case, I'll make him stop loving Watford. Yeah, that's what I'll do. Then he'll just vanish.'

'Ha!' Derek interjected. 'Falling out of love with Watford doesn't make you vanish from Hornet Heaven, Mr Sargent, sir. If it did, Walter Mazzarri's football would have completely emptied the place last season! Ha!'

Freddie swore at the boy and told him to shut up. Derek gulped and looked a little tearful.

'The Plastic's got to go,' Freddie insisted. 'Trying to make him vanish by making him fall out of love with Watford is definitely worth a shot. So, come on: any ideas how?'

'Freddie,' Bill said gently, 'I have to say I think you're being a little harsh on the new arrival.'

This time Freddie swore at Bill.

Bill's eyelashes fluttered, flustered, behind his spectacles.

'For crying out loud!' Freddie yelled. 'Do I have to do everything myself round here? Right. You watch me. I won't rest until the Plastic's gone.'

*   *   *

Freddie headed for The Gallery — the swanky restaurant in the south west corner of the stadium. He needed some peace and quiet to think up a plan. On the way in, he met Walter Coles coming out. Walter was a free-scoring Watford Rovers team-mate who, in 1891/92, scored 60 goals in just 26 games.

'Blimey, Freddie, me old mate,' Walter said. 'What's wrong? Your face is longer than when we lost 9-1 at home to Crewe Alexandra in April 1892.'

'Yeah, well, I've just found out there's a Plastic in Hornet Heaven.'

'Ha! Just one? The place has been full of them since 1896! Any Watford fan who wasn't there for the club when we started out in Southern League Division Two is just a Glory Hunter! A despicable Johnny-Come-Lately!'

Walter walked off, laughing to himself as if he'd said something funny. But Freddie couldn't help thinking that his old team-mate had actually made a decent point.

Freddie went over to the bar and sat down to try and

think up a plan for getting the Plastic out of Hornet Heaven. But the man next to him at the bar started talking to him.

'Gawd,' the man said. 'Did you see the penalty Gomes gave away against Liverpool? He's a liability. We need to ship him out.'

'Sorry, mate,' Freddie replied. 'Normally I'd chat, but I need to sit quietly and think.'

'We're having a terrible transfer window. I can't believe we've started the season with no cover at left-back.'

'Mate, I don't need this at the moment.'

'How is Amrabat still at the club? He's Championship at best.'

'Blimey, you're a Moaner, mate. You really know how to suck all the joy out of being a Watford fan, don't you. Five minutes with you and no-one would want to be a Horn anymore… Wait… Perfect… You're just the man I need. Come with me.'

*　*　*

Freddie took the Moaner to the atrium and sat him down on the yellow sofas next to the Plastic Fan. Then Freddie hid behind the programme shelves to watch what would happen.

Before long, Bill Mainwood walked past and saw Freddie.

Bill said: 'Hello, Freddie. Why have you got your fingers in your ears?... Freddie?… Freddie!!'

Freddie finally noticed Bill and said: 'What? Oh. It's you. I'm making sure I don't hear this Moaner. If I do, I might fall out of love with Watford, and vanish from Hornet Heaven. That's what I'm trying to make happen to the Plastic.'

Freddie kept his fingers in his ears. Bill stopped and listened in to the conversation that was developing between the Moaner and the Plastic on the sofas.

'And another thing,' the Moaner said. 'We never put defenders on the posts at corners.'

The Plastic clapped his hand genially on the Moaner's shoulder and said: 'Hey, good buddy, there's no need to moan. You want to get behind the Horns like the rest of us.'

'Etienne Capoue is lazy,' the Moaner continued regardless. 'The sponsor's logo on the shirt is too big. The holes in the nets are the wrong shape. Harry The Hornet has been doing the same dance moves for years.'

'Come on, good buddy, be positive,' the Plastic said. 'We've just proved we're as good as Liverpool. What an amazing feeling for a Watford fan. It's why I love the big games so much — when the Horns are challenging at the highest level.'

Meanwhile, over by the shelves, Bill whispered to Freddie: 'You know, I think you may be wrong about this fellow you call the Plastic.'

'I can't hear what you're saying.'

Bill said slightly louder: 'I think he genuinely loves the Horns.'

Freddie sang to himself: 'La la la la la la la la. I can't hear you.'

Bill frowned. He thought Freddie seemed rather prejudiced against the so-called Plastic. He carried on listening in to the conversation. But not for long. When the Moaner started banging on about zonal marking at corners, Bill stuffed his own fingers into his ears.

And when the Moaner said that Watford needed to get Fernando Forestieri back from Sheffield Wednesday, every single person in the atrium jammed their fingers in their ears — including the Plastic.

Freddie seethed. His plan had failed. He went off to come up with something else.

* * *

Freddie went back to the programme office and spoke to Derek Garston again.

'You've got to help me get rid of him,' Freddie insisted.

'But why, Mr Sargent, sir? I still don't understand what's so terrible about him. He's a fan, isn't he?'

'Plastics are bad for the club.'

'Well, actually, Mr Sargent, sir, you could argue the opposite. So-called Plastics bring the club extra income that can be invested in activities across the whole community. In that sense, they're good for everyone, Mr Sargent, sir.'

'Shut up and listen. I've got a new plan. I want to show the Plastic that Big Clubs aren't as great as he thinks they are. When he realises that they aren't actually big and clever at all, he'll lose interest and clear off out of Hornet Heaven.'

'Ooh, I like the sound of that, Mr Sargent, sir.'

'Really? You think it's a good plan?'

'I don't really know, Mr Sargent, sir, but what fun to expose the Sky Sports era as an over-hyped sham! As a money-thieving manipulation of ordinary fans' perceptions! As a morally empty circus of—'

'Alright, boy. Don't get carried away. I just need you to suggest some games that will show him that the Big Clubs aren't so glamorous after all.'

'Well, that won't be too hard, Mr Sargent, sir. How about our 5-1 win at Stamford Bridge in May 1986? Chelsea were awful back then. Only 12,017 people bothered to turn up and watch.'

'No good. David Bardsley was a complete and utter god that day. The Plastic will be distracted by how good the Orns were, not how terrible Chelsea were.'

'Ah, in that case I know just the game, Mr Sargent, sir. Chelsea v Watford on Tuesday 29th March 1988. Both teams were getting relegated from the top division. They were both complete and utter… Oh dear. Mr Mainwood won't allow me to use the word I've got in mind, Mr Sargent, sir… Ah, I know. I'll use Watford rhyming slang instead. They were both complete and utter Assombalonga.'

'Complete Britt? Sounds perfect, boy. Two programmes, please.'

* * *

Back in the atrium, Freddie took two programmes to the yellow sofa where the Plastic was sitting.

'Oi! Plastic!' Freddie said. 'Watford are playing at Chelsea. Want to go?'

'Hey, good buddy,' the Plastic replied. 'That's a pleasant surprise. I thought we weren't playing Chelsea until October.'

'What? Oh. I see. Yeah, well, it got moved forward. For the telly. Bloody Sky Sports. They've created a morally empty circus of… …something or other: Derek will fill you in. Anyway, the game's just starting. I've got programmes for both of us.'

'Ooh, let's have a look. I want to see their squad for 2017/18. I bet it's phenomenal.' '

Oi! Get your plastic hands off! You can't look at the programme until we're in the stadium.'

The Plastic got to his feet undeterred. He said: 'Hey, this is great, good buddy. I thought you didn't approve of me.'

'Come on, let's get a move on. Hazard's in their team. You don't want to miss him.'

'Hazard? I heard he was injured.'

'He's playing. I swear on my afterlife.'

The Plastic was so excited, he ran to the ancient turnstile.

* * *

Freddie and the Plastic arrived, in pouring rain, at Stamford Bridge in March 1988. They stood in the roofless away end of a stadium that was totally dilapidated apart from the giant East Stand.

As the game kicked off, the Plastic asked: 'Hey, good buddy, I don't get it. Where am I?'

Freddie muttered: 'On your way out of Hornet Heaven, mate.'

'What's that, good buddy? What d'you say?'

'I said we're at Stamford Bridge.'

'No way, good buddy. We can't be. I mean, check out the state of the pitch. It looks better suited to girl-on-girl mud-wrestling than football. I'm surprised the players aren't wearing bikinis.'

'No! Shut up! Don't make me imagine that! Sir Nigel Gibbs is out there! That's sacrilege! Agh! I can't un-imagine that now!'

'Wait a moment. Nigel Gibbs? Didn't he play for us years ago?'

'He certainly did. I've brought you to the past. 1988.'

'Hey, that's not fair, good buddy. You swore on your afterlife that Hazard would be playing.'

'He is.'

'What? Eden Hazard didn't play for Chelsea when Stamford Bridge was a… a toilet like this.'

'I was talking about Micky Hazard — their chubby number 8 over there, sitting in that puddle. Did you think I meant Eden? I'm so sorry for any confusion.'

'Whoa. This is totally uncool, good buddy. I'm here under false pretences.'

'Ain't that the truth.'

'I mean, where have all the stands gone? Where are the fans?'

'There's only 11,240 paying customers. Pretty poor for a Big Club, eh?'

'And why are there two people watching from inside an old grey Ford Escort next to the corner flag? What's that about? Seriously, this is totally Mickey Mouse.'

'Exactly. And it's only four years before the Premier League came along. Makes you think, doesn't it?'

Freddie looked at the Plastic. The Plastic looked genuinely shell-shocked.

Freddie smiled. His plan to make the Plastic see the big clubs for what they were — and quit Hornet Heaven as a result — seemed to be working.

After a while, in the pouring rain, after Stuart Rimmer put Watford 1-0 up with a weak shot that skidded under the Chelsea keeper, the Plastic said: 'I feel terrible. I can't believe what a fool I've been. I've been played. Everything I thought Chelsea stood for is obviously just a billion-pound make-over.'

'Perfect. I'm glad you can see it at last.'

'Coming here, it's obvious. Big clubs aren't special. Everything that attracted me to them is just a veneer. I've been so stupid. As a small club fan, I wanted the prestige of the big clubs to rub off on me when, really, underneath it all, the big clubs arc just... football teams like any other.'

Freddie grinned and clapped his hands.

'Great. That's that, then. We can go now. Come on. Let's go back through the ancient turnstile. Obviously — now that you won't be wanting to go to games against the big clubs — there's nothing of interest in a Watford paradise for a Plastic like you. Once you're back on

Occupation Road, you can let yourself out of Hornet Heaven and leave us proper fans to get on with it.'

Freddie strode off through the rain. Before long, though, he realised that the Plastic wasn't following him. He turned back to see what was going on. The Plastic was still in the same spot on the terrace, in his pin-striped suit, drenched.

The Plastic called out through the downpour: 'But… But I don't want to quit Hornet Heaven.'

Freddie strode back over immediately. He said: 'You've got to leave. There's nothing for you here.'

'But seeing the truth about the big clubs hasn't made me want to leave.'

'What? Don't say that. It must have done.'

'Quite the opposite.'

'Oh God. What are you saying? That I've brought you here and it's made you want to go to more games than ever?

'Exactly.'

Freddie closed his eyes in the pouring rain and said: 'Britt!'

* * *

Freddie stomped back through the ancient turnstile, furious that his plan had backfired. He noticed the Plastic was following him this time. He stopped on Occupation Road and said: 'I don't get it. How has that trip made someone like you want to go to more games?'

The Plastic replied: 'The thing is, good buddy, it made me realise I've been supporting Watford in the wrong way. I thought the big clubs were the clubs with all the kudos. But if they're only football teams like any other, then my own club is just as prestigious. I should feel a lot more pride in supporting Watford, whoever they're playing.'

On hearing this, Freddie's anger started to seep away a little. The Plastic was sounding a bit more like a proper fan.

'Yeah, well,' he said. 'You blooming well *should* feel pride whoever we're playing. I always have. Even when we've been playing Grimsby Town. All 46 times.'

The Plastic said: 'I want to feel pride at every game. I think I can.'

Freddie stared at the Plastic and felt his own attitude beginning to soften. He'd always hated Johnny-Come-Lately Glory-Boys because they were getting the best bits of supporting Watford without having to earn them the hard way like he had. He'd been devoted to Watford at every level of the game since the 1880s. He'd played for the club before it had been good enough to join any kind of league. He'd scored goals against teams that Johnny-Come-Lately Glory-Boys would never have heard of: Old Foresters, Champion Hill, A.T.B Dunn's XI.

His degree of commitment meant that, over the years, he'd always felt personally cheated by fans turning up just for the good times. And yet now, standing drenched on Occupation Road with one of them, he was beginning to think that, if they could feel pride in Watford, then maybe Plastics weren't so detestable after all.

Freddie looked at the man in front of him and felt a bit bad about himself for having been so extreme in his views. He said: 'So. Are you going to watch us at Bournemouth on Saturday? You might not like it. Tinpot club, they are.'

'Wow, good buddy, that's a tough one to start with. There's no kudos in playing the likes of them. They're a tiny club. Miniscule.'

'Microscopic.'

The Plastic swallowed hard and said: 'But I'll be

proud to be there, supporting the Horns.'

Freddie smiled. He reckoned he definitely had been too harsh on the bloke. He patted the Plastic on the shoulder and said: 'Good bloke. Good bloke. See you there.'

*   *   *

On the Saturday, Freddie was in the packed Watford section at Bournemouth's Vitality Stadium. The atmosphere among the Category A and A+ away fans — there were no real-world Plastics here — was electric.

Throughout the first half, Freddie kept an eye out for the Plastic but couldn't see him. He had a good look round at half time too. In the end, he gave up and tore himself off a strip for being stupid. Plastics obviously couldn't change their ways. Why had he ever thought they could?

In the second half, he paid full attention to the game. Watford were playing brilliantly. In the 73rd minute, Nathaniel Chalobah played the ball into Andre Gray behind Bournemouth's defence. Gray crossed. Richarlison, Watford's new Brazilian striker, scored.

Freddie found himself in a massive bundle, hugging

strangers again, planting bristly kisses left right and centre. It didn't matter to Freddie who Watford were playing — he just loved watching the Horns win. He ended up several rows closer to the front of the stand. Suddenly he saw the Plastic next to him.

'Oh. Right,' he said. 'You're here.'

'Hey, good buddy. Yah. I'm here.'

'I thought maybe you couldn't hack it. You know, what with Watford playing a team as small and irrelevant as Bournemouth.'

'Actually, good buddy, I prepared myself carefully during the week. I went to watch some old Watford games against nothing teams.

'Nothing teams like Bournemouth?'

'Before Bournemouth even existed, actually. I went back to your playing days. You know — when Watford were a nothing team too.'

The Plastic winked at Freddie.

Freddie said: 'Oi! Watch it, you!'

'And I didn't stop there,' the Plastic continued. 'I went back right to the very beginning.'

'Really? I'm impressed. Who did you see?'

The Plastic took a deep breath and recited: Wheeler, Horton, Capell, Grover, Valentine, Hurndall, Waterman,

Horton, Smith, Christmas, Grace.'

Freddie stared at the Plastic in amazement. He felt quite moved by what he'd just heard. He said: 'Blimey. That really does make you a Horn. Not a Plastic at all. A proper Horn.'

Freddie took his new friend's hand and shook it warmly. Then they watched the final minutes of Watford's superb away performance. In the 86th minute, they saw Etienne Capoue extend one of his long action-figure legs and fire home a shot from outside the box.

Freddie and his new Hornet friend screamed with joy. They leapt. They hugged.

As they bounced around the terrace in their embrace, Freddie noticed he didn't feel physically sick this time. They were just two Watford fans together, excited about their club; proud of their club.

Neither of them were plastic, he now knew. They were both plasma. And yet the love they both felt for the Horns was as real as anything anywhere on heaven and earth.

THE END

12

NEVER TOO HIGH, NEVER TOO LOW

EARTH SEASON 2017/18

'You know what, Lamper?' Henry Grover said. 'I hate international breaks.'

'Oi!' Lamper replied. 'Don't beat yourself up over it! Let *me* beat you up!'

'They're so boring. International breaks mean no excitement for two whole weeks.'

'Then let's get a ruck going. Come on! Bring it on!'

'That's a terribly kind offer, Lamper. But I think I'd prefer to wait and get my fix of excitement in the usual way — when this tedious interruption to our fixture list is over.'

'What did you say? Get your fix?'

'Sorry. It's an idiomatic expression. It means to obtain something compulsively sought. Commonly used in the context of—'

'I know what it means, you muppet. It's given me an idea, that's all. I've just thought of the perfect way to stop people in Hornet Heaven from being bored.'

'Really, Lamper? That sounds splendid.'

Lamper had a huge broken-toothed grin on his face. He said: 'Yeah. I'm going to make everyone bleeding love this international break. You watch me.'

* * *

Two days later, Bill Mainwood and his 13-year-old assistant, Derek Garston, were in the Hornet Heaven programme office.

Bill sighed: 'I wish we'd won the Brighton game on Saturday, my boy. If we'd won it by a couple of goals, we'd have gone second in the Premier League. That would have given us some excitement to carry us through this interminable international break.'

Derek chirped: 'Would you like one of my yellow sweeties to cheer you up, sir?'

'No thank you, my boy,' Bill replied, and continued

moaning: 'The lack of fixtures is a real bore now we're in the Premier League. They came thick and fast in the Championship.'

'I know, sir,' Derek said. He swallowed one of his sweeties and continued: 'It's alright for people in the land of the living, sir. The media keeps them excited between matches. They get transfer rumours, sir! Scandals, sir! Twitter-spats, sir! Up here, we don't get to see or hear any of that, sir. It's not fair, sir.'

'Well, I'm afraid I don't approve of media hype, young man. It's all manufactured to feed fans' appetites. At least up here in Hornet Heaven we've got the old games to keep going back to.'

'Good point, sir. In fact, I'm ready for another one now, sir. I want to see a particularly exciting game. Let's go to the Leicester Play-Off semi, sir!'

* * *

Bill and Derek went out onto Occupation Road and through the ancient turnstile.

In added time, the amazing climax of the Leicester game began to unfold.

'It's not fair, sir,' Derek said. 'Knockaert obviously

dived, sir. If he scores this, I'll…'

The crowd around them roared.

'Almunia's saved it, sir! And again, sir!'

Bill said: 'I don't need a running commentary, thank you. We've been back here to watch this game dozens of times before.'

The crowd roared louder.

'Look, sir! Go, Ikechi, go! I've never seen anything like this before!'

'Calm down, my boy. You can't pretend it's the first time we've seen it.'

'Hogg's going to score, sir! Wait! He's laying it back to… DEEEEENNNNNEEEEYY!'

The crowd exploded in joy.

'Oh my God, sir!' Derek shrieked. 'Oh my God! This is incredible! I don't remember seeing anything like it, sir!'

'Honestly, Derek. You've seen this very goal. Dozens of times. For goodness's sake. Are you on drugs or something?'

'Yes, sir!' Derek replied ecstatically.

'What?

'I took a pill earlier, sir!'

'But—'

Derek cried out shrilly: 'I'm on mind-altering drugs, sir, and it's amazing!'

*   *   *

Bill carried his young assistant into the atrium and laid the boy down on one of the yellow leather sofas. For a while he kept watch. Then, when the thirteen-year-old fell into an exhausted sleep after his drug-induced high, Bill went off to find Henry Grover, the man who founded Watford Rovers in 1881. The Father Of The Club was at the programme shelves.

Bill said: 'I'm so glad I've found you, Henry. I wanted to tell you as soon as I could. Someone is manufacturing drugs in Hornet Heaven.'

Henry glanced around the atrium. He said quietly: 'Shh, Bill. I know. But keep your voice down. The last thing I want is for other residents to find out.'

'Oh. Right. Very wise. And have you discovered who it is?'

'Oh yes. I know exactly who it is.'

'Good. Because he's pushing his drugs onto innocent children. It has to stop.'

'Absolutely. We definitely can't have that…

There'd be less to go round for us grown-ups!'

Henry held out two small yellow pills in his palm. He whispered delightedly: 'Don't say anything, old chap, or everyone will want one. Football fans crave *any* kind of stimulation during international breaks.'

Bill stared, horrified, as Henry popped one of the pills into his mouth and offered him the other.

'No thank you, Henry!'

'Oh, Bill. Don't be such a stick-in-the-mud. This little beauty delivers exhilaration of a kind you can't get anywhere else during these fortnights of enforced boredom.'

'I don't want my excitement artificially induced. Watching Watford gives me all the natural euphoria I need… Well, sometimes it does… …Every now and then, anyway.'

'You see, Bill? This pill fills those gaps. It makes a trip back to watch an old game exactly that — a total trip, daddy-o.'

Henry took two copies of a programme from one of the shelves and headed towards the atrium's exit.

'Come on. I'll show you. This trip is going to be…. far out, man!'

* * *

On Occupation Road, on the way to the ancient turnstile, Bill refused another offer of a pill. He said: 'The international break only lasts two weeks. We should all just wait for the away game at Southampton for any new excitement. We need to be patient, Henry.'

'Oh, for goodness's sake, Bill, don't be such a square,' Henry replied. 'Have some fun for once.'

'I do have fun. In moderation. Only yesterday I re-arranged a whole pile of programmes in alphabetical order.'

'Well, in just a moment we'll be at the UEFA Cup home game against Kaiserslautern in 1983. This will be proper fun. It was the first ever European game at Vicarage Road. An absolutely incredible night. You remember what happened, I take it?'

'Of course I do. We'd lost the away leg 3-1 in Germany, but we were ahead on aggregate inside 10 minutes of the home leg.'

'Exactly. Those first ten minutes were simply unforgettable.'

Henry took Bill through the ancient turnstile. They arrived inside Vicarage Road on September 28th 1983.

The floodlights shone down from a black sky.

'Right,' Henry said. 'I can't wait to find out what happens.'

'What? But you know what happens. We discussed it only a moment ago. You said it was unforgettable.'

'Ha! Dear old Bill! Don't you know how this drug works?'

'No. I've got no interest in artificial highs.'

'Well, more fool you, old son. You see, with this drug, as soon as you go through the ancient turnstile you lose all knowledge of how the game you're revisiting turns out. It's like watching it for the first time. It's glorious.'

'Goodness. That must be what Derek was experiencing when we went back to the 2013 Leicester play-off semi-final.'

'No idea what game you're talking about, Bill. Right now, thanks to this drug, I don't know anything that happens to Watford on or after September 28th 1983. I possess no knowledge that could spoil my pure enjoyment of this game. I'm going to be living this game, not re-living it. Come on, let's go and stand behind the goal.'

'But I haven't taken a pill.'

'Then you simply won't enjoy it as much as I will. Now, let's get this party started.'

Bill went and stood with Henry under the scoreboard on the Vicarage Road terrace. When the teams came out, he was pleased to be reminded that Watford had been wearing black shorts on the night, not the usual 1980s red. It wasn't a particularly exciting thing. It was just something that gave him a deep satisfaction that all was right with the world.

The game started. After four minutes, John Barnes flicked the ball into the path of young Ian Richardson. Richardson controlled it deftly and slotted it into the corner of the Kaiserslautern net for the first goal. Bedlam broke out on the terrace around them. Bill definitely enjoyed it — experiencing it for the umpteenth time — but not nearly as much as Henry. Henry jumped onto Bill's back and screamed with joy.

'Get in!' Henry yelled. 'Oh my God, Bill! It's on! We could actually do this! This is amazing!'

Six minutes later, Nigel Callaghan back-heeled the ball to the overlapping Charlie Palmer. Palmer sent in a low cross. The Kaiserslautern keeper pushed the ball out. It hit one of his defenders and flew into the net. Watford were ahead in the tie, and there was pandemonium on the terrace again. Bill felt Henry on his shoulders this time. Henry was in his long johns, whirling his trousers around his head, in complete rapture.

Bill looked up at Henry. He wanted what Henry was having.

But something felt wrong about it. Being able to enjoy the original euphoria of an amazing match time and time again felt like cheating.

Bill looked up at Henry. Henry was trying to remove his long-johns so he could swing those around his head too.

Bill asked: 'Are you enjoying yourself up there, Henry?'

Henry replied euphorically: 'I'm totally stoked, man.'

Bill made a decision. He didn't want to be a killjoy, but the dishonesty of watching old games as though they were new made him feel as though the integrity of Hornet Heaven depended on his taking urgent action. He had to do something.

He said: 'So, um, tell me, Henry. Where can I get hold of what you're on?'

Henry leaned down and whispered the answer into Bill's ear.

Bill nodded.

He was now on a mission to shut down the Hornet Heaven drugs chain.

* * *

Bill made his way through the murky half-light of the nether regions of Occupation Road where new arrivals materialised and where Lamper, the former hooligan turned Hornet Heaven chief steward, usually lurked in the shadows. He called out: 'Lamper? Lamper?'

Bill wanted to ask the chief steward to provide him with protection as he took on what might prove to be a violent drugs gang. But Lamper wasn't to be found.

Bill rounded the corner and walked along behind the Rookery stand, following Henry's directions. He felt scared. At the far end, through the gloom, he saw a wide staircase with six columns of steps divided by silver-coloured handrails. Cautiously, he descended. At the bottom, on his right, he saw a heavy-duty metal cage guarding a yellow door. Bill had never been here before. The cage suggested danger, but he couldn't turn back now if he wanted to put an end to drugs trafficking in Hornet Heaven.

There was a dark grey metal door set into the fencing of the cage. Bill pulled at it. It was locked.

He wasn't sure what to do. He looked through the fencing at the yellow wooden door. Suddenly he noticed it edge open — just a crack. A voice said: 'Who is it?'

'Oh. Hello,' Bill replied nervously. 'It's Bill Mainwood. From the programme office.'

'The authorities, eh?' the voice said. 'Piss off, or you'll get a kicking.'

The yellow door shut.

Bill, still outside the cage, called out: 'No. I'm here unofficially. I want to, er, um….'

Bill braced himself to lie. He winced as he announced: 'I want to score some serious shit.'

The door opened again. Warily, a stocky skinhead — in his 1980s casual gear of Lacoste polo shirt and Farah slacks — peered out. Through the gloom, Bill recognised the figure's scarred, shaven, slightly mis-shapen, skull.

'Oh,' Bill said. 'It's you. Hello, Lamper.'

'Oi!' Lamper hissed. 'No names! This is a covert operation, you numpty!'

Lamper stepped forward and unlocked the metal cage door. He beckoned Bill through. Then he started to pat Bill down.

'Can't take no chances, can I?' he said. 'I was always Hornet Heaven's top boy but now I'm the street lord. The Frank Lucas. The Pablo Escobar.'

Lamper finished patting Bill down. He said: 'Welcome to the sugarhouse!'

Bill took a deep breath and stepped through the yellow door into a subterranean cavern.

The underground space was windowless and airless, with artificial strip lighting. The flooring was pale brick. There were red columns and yellow walls. On the walls were banners that Bill recognised from Saturday's Premier League home game against Brighton and Hove Albion. Written on the banners, columns, and floor was a date. Suddenly Bill realised what this place was. Lamper was using the 1881 bunker as his drugs den.

'After a little bit of ecstasy, then, are ya?' Lamper asked.

Bill thought about revealing his true intentions straightaway. But he decided to play along for a bit longer.

'Is that what you call your yellow pill? Ecstasy?'

'Course not. Ecstasy is what it gives you at old Watford games. My little yellow pill is called…

Bogside.'

'Bogside? Why?'

'Cos, back in the 70s, I was in the Bogside firm — and it was the most exciting thing ever. You never knew what was going to happen next. And when it all kicked off… now that was ecstasy.'

Bill stepped further into the bunker — to establish the full extent of Lamper's drugs operation before he closed it down. On the far side, a machine was whirring. He went over to take a look.

'So,' he said, 'this is where you "cook up", is it?'

'Nah, mate. I don't "cook up". I'm far more sophisticated than that. The pills are plasma microchips. I bullied Roy in IT into showing me how to make them. They communicate with the technology behind the ancient turnstile — to alter your experience.'

Bill had seen and heard enough. He said: 'Well, I'm afraid that's where I take issue. Now listen to me, Lamper. The experience of watching Watford is all we have in Hornet Heaven. Tampering with it is dangerous. Who knows where it will lead. I insist you stop making and distributing your evil candy.'

'Oi! What's your problem? No-one's ever had a bad trip on Bogside.'

'I'm sorry, but what you're doing has to stop. It's wrong.'

'How is it wrong?'

'Do you really want me to list the ways? Well, for starters, amazing Watford moments are like a profound religious experience. We must feel them as they actually are — with our minds pure, clear, and unaltered. '

'Gawd, you're a buzz-killer. So you'd ban beer, would ya?'

'And there's a right way of doing things in Hornet Heaven. The old games are for reflection and nostalgia. Not for having your mind blown. That's for the new games to do.'

'Are you finishing any time soon, mate?'

'And what does it say about our Watford paradise if we take drugs to make our afterlife more exciting? It says Hornet Heaven isn't heavenly enough. We'll become dissatisfied with our eternal existence. And that would be terrible.'

'We could probably borrow the media room if you wanna do a full presentation, mate, with Powerpoint slides and that.'

'But it goes much deeper too. The memories of the joy I had at all those old matches aren't just Watford memories. They're a part of my own history, part of me. Wiping them from my mind, albeit temporarily, would be messing around with who I am as a person. That has to be dangerous.'

'Blinking flip! This international break is going to be finished before you are!'

'At the end of the day, these pills are yet another thing that's been manufactured to get fans excited. They're like transfer tittle-tattle in the land of the living. They're designed to exploit the appetite that the charade of modern football has—'

Lamper started clapping.

'Brilliant, mate. Brilliant,' he said and stopped clapping. 'But saddle down your high horse, because I can undo all that with one question. Do you want some? Do ya?'

Bill stepped back a little. 'Now, now, Lamper. I'm not interested in violence. I simply want to—'

'Nah, you muppet. Want some drugs, do ya? Some Bogside. I bet you've never even tried it.'

Lamper pressed a small yellow pill into Bill's hand. Bill couldn't help staring at it. Suddenly, now he was holding it, he was awestruck at how something so small could turn old games into new games and bring such extraordinary joy. The promise of ecstasy was right there in the palm of his hand. He could almost feel it already. He wavered.

'No… I…'

'Go on, mate. You deserve it. You know you do. All Watford fans deserve it after what we had to suffer under Walter Mazzarri last season.'

Bill had already forgotten last season because he was so pleased with how things had started going under Marco Silva. But, with the pill in his palm, it felt as though Lamper had a very decent point.

'Well, when you put it like that…'

'Exactly. After Wally, you deserve rapture on tap, mate. Today. Tomorrow. The day after. Every day. For eternity.'

Bill gazed at the tab. It was tiny. Taking it would be so easy.

Now he looked at Lamper. Lamper was much more street-wise than he was. He felt a ridiculous prude by comparison — with his schoolma'am attitude to drugs.

And anyway, he asked himself, what was so wrong with Watford fans experiencing extreme bliss? Wasn't extreme bliss the whole point of an afterlife paradise?

He apologised to Lamper for the intrusion, pocketed

the pill, and left the 1881 bunker.

Bill Mainwood was suddenly feeling an appetite he'd never felt before.

* * *

In the atrium, Bill stood and stared at the programme shelves. Stretching far into the distance, the programmes in front of him represented the full playing history of Watford Football Club since 1881. He'd been to all of the very best matches already — many times — but the drug in his pocket would turn one of them into a virgin experience. He was twitching with excitement.

But he couldn't decide which game to choose. He was pretty sure he should opt for the single most euphoric experience as a Watford fan — to get the very most from the pill — but he couldn't work out which game that would be. Was it winning promotion to the top flight for the first time in 1982? Or reaching the FA Cup Final in 1984? Or winning at Wembley in 1999? He felt his appetite growing.

As he contemplated the possibilities, he started to wish he had more than one pill. After all, there were more than 5,000 games available. If he went to each one, in order, and took a pill before he went through the ancient turnstile each time, he could live Watford's entire existence as a series of first-time experiences — from the very first friendly games in Vicarage Meadow to the most recent Premier League game at Vicarage Road. He'd be able to experience the whole 136-year story, game by game, without spoilers. He couldn't think of anything more wonderful. He'd completely forgotten his earlier conviction that no-one should interfere with the integrity of Hornet Heaven.

Suddenly, he heard a voice behind him. It was Henry.

'Ah. Bill. I hear you've fixed yourself up with some stash. Seen the light, have you, old son? Joining us ravers, are you?'

Bill turned and saw that Henry's pupils were hugely dilated. This only made Bill more excited at what lay in store.

Bill said: 'I've got myself a sweet little tab of Bogside. You know what they say: "Live fast, die young."'

'Even though you're 92 and you're already dead?' Henry replied. 'Excellent attitude, old chap. And such a very good example to set your young assistant, Derek, may I say.'

'Oh. Yes. I was a bit worried that some people might think a junkie is a bad role model for a thirteen-year-old boy.'

'Well, they'd be wrong. Poor Derek died young before he even had the chance to live fast. That lad deserves to snort, swallow or shoot up all the narcotics he can lay his hands on.'

'Henry! That's a bit much. Are you still high after Kaiserslautern?'

'I… er… I might be, old thing. A little bit. But it's jolly well time you were too. Come on, Bill, pop your pill and let's find you a game. I think I may know just the one. You'll be buzzing your tits off in no time.'

'I'm ready. Bring it on.'

Bill pulled the yellow pill out of his pocket. He looked at it and had one last moment of doubt.

'Are you sure there are no adverse effects?'

'Oh, Bill. You've seen the joy Bogside has given Derek and me. What could possibly go wrong?'

Bill popped the tab of Bogside into his mouth and shouted: 'Youuuuu Orrrrrns!'

*　*　*

On Occupation Road, outside the ancient turnstile, Bill said to Henry: 'Golly, I'm so excited, Henry. I've been back to this game dozens of times over the years. But when you already know the score it doesn't quite feel the same as it originally did. Revisiting the game without this drug just doesn't recapture the sheer unexpectedness of Watford 7 Southampton 1.'

'Absolutely,' Henry replied. 'It was the most astonishing result in Watford history. You're in for the ride of your afterlife, old chap.'

'Goodness. I do hope the pill works. I don't feel any different at the moment.'

'Don't worry. Bogside kicks in when you go through the turnstile. Once you're in the ground, you'll find you have no knowledge of anything that happened to Watford on or after September 2nd 1980. Come on, in you go.'

They passed through the ancient turnstile. The floodlights were on and there was a very decent crowd of 16,000. Henry felt jealous of what Bill was about to experience. He took Bill onto the Vicarage Road terrace, beneath the scoreboard, to make sure his old friend felt the full effect.

But when the Watford team ran onto the pitch in their shiny yellow shirts and shiny red shorts, Bill asked: 'Er… Which team is that, Henry?'

Henry frowned.

Bill had another question: 'And what's the name of this ground? I've never been here before.'

'What?'

'I mean, football's alright, but I couldn't really say I'm a big fan of any particular team.'

'Bill! What's happened to you? This is Watford! Your team!'

'Watford? Never heard of them. Oh, well. Let's hope it's a good match for the neutral.'

As the match kicked off, Henry tried to work out what had happened. Somehow, he realised, the pill must have erased Bill's knowledge of anything that had happened to Watford *before* September 2nd 1980, as well as on or after.

In the tenth minute of the game, Henry watched Bill's lukewarm reaction as Malcolm Poskett scored Watford's first goal.

'Hmm,' Bill said. 'Nothing particularly special about that.'

Henry realised that Bill must have no idea what the

score had been in the first leg at Southampton. He informed Bill that Watford had lost the first game 4-0.

Bill replied: 'Well, that makes this a complete waste of time. And even if there was a surprise result, I don't really care for either team. Shall we go?'

Henry persuaded Bill to stay. They watched Ray Train make it 2-0 and Martin Patching make it 3-0. The crowd around them were beginning to believe in the impossible, but Bill seemed more interested in the pigeons on top of the Shrodells Stand.

Henry began to be upset for Bill. The drug wasn't giving his old friend a euphoric experience at all. In fact, it was making Bill enjoy the occasion less than he would have done if he'd come to the game normally.

After Southampton pulled one back, Bill didn't see Ian Bolton's penalty putting Watford 4-1 up because he had his back to the game while he read the adverts on the scoreboard.

This was the point at which Henry began to realise, with horror, the true extent of what had happened to Bill. Thanks to the drug, Bill wasn't a Watford fan anymore. He had no Watford memories. No passion for the club. No loyalty. No love. The drug had turned him into an empty ghost. His soul contained none of the depth and richness that decades of supporting Watford had put there. Bill Mainwood wasn't Bill Mainwood.

Henry stood in front of Bill and put his hands on Bill's shoulders. He said: 'Bill, my old friend. I can't bear to see you like this.'

Bill said: 'I don't think much of those silly jumping men on the scoreboard.'

'I need to take you away from here,' Henry continued. 'Get you back to being yourself.'

'I do rather like Watford's red shorts, though,' Bill said.

'No you don't, Bill!' Henry cried. 'You like *black* shorts! You're wrong, of course, but you do. That's one of things I love about you. I want you back, Bill. The real you.'

Henry took Bill by the arm and led him down off the terrace.

As Ross Jenkins levelled the tie with Watford's fifth goal — and 16,000 real-world Watford fans experienced a euphoria of an intensity that most had never felt before — Henry and Bill, feeling no excitement whatsoever, went back through the ancient turnstile onto Occupation Road.

* * *

'Open up!' Henry shouted. 'Lamper! Open up immediately!'

Henry grabbed the wires of the cage outside the 1881 bunker and shook them angrily. There was no answer from behind the yellow wooden door.

Henry said to Bill: 'I'm furious with him. What happened to you was unforgivable.'

'It's my own fault,' Bill said. 'I should never have dabbled with drugs.'

'But are you sure you're OK again — now that you're this side of the ancient turnstile? Let me check. Who scored this club's first ever hat-trick?'

'Freddie Sargent on March 21st 1885.'

'Excellent. That's the knowledge of an extremely well-informed Horn. And who did Miguel Britos get sent off for fouling last week?'

'That horrid little Anthony Knockaert.'

'Good. The attitude of a true Watford fan. You've made a full recovery.'

Henry banged on the cage and shouted for Lamper again.

Soon the yellow door inside the cage opened.

'Alright, alright!' Lamper said. 'Keep your flipping hair on! And don't call me Lamper. I'm Pablo now. The drugs kingpin.'

Lamper came out and unlocked the metal cage door. Henry stormed through into the gaudy yellow 1881 bunker. Bill and Lamper followed.

Inside, Henry grabbed Lamper by the collar of his Lacoste polo shirt and said: 'Your drugs are an evil. Bogside is a menace to society!'

'Well, you've changed your tune,' Lamper retorted. 'You've been loving your Bogside.'

'Bill has just had a bad trip,' Henry continued. 'He went to a game and… suddenly he wasn't a Watford fan.'

'What?'

'It's… It's… unconscionable! Not supporting Watford is the worst possible thing that could happen to anyone!'

'Nah. He must have got hold of a different drug — from someone else. Maybe some other pusher is trying to muscle in on my patch.'

'What? With a drug people can take to forget they're Watford fans? When would anyone ever want to do that?'

'I bet the drug's called "Bassini".'

Bill interjected: 'No, Lamper. It was definitely Bogside I took.'

Lamper replied: 'Well, you look alright to me. No harm done, eh?'

'No!' Henry cried. 'No, no, no! I founded this club and I won't allow what's going on. I've seen what a bad trip did to Bill and it was terrifying. It may only have been temporary in this instance, but what if the effect had been permanent? Not being a Watford fan altered Bill's personality. It stole his soul. He had no identity. It removed the reason for his existence. Your drug has no place in Hornet Heaven, Lamper.'

Henry looked across the bunker. He let go of Lamper and marched over to Lamper's machine. 'Is this what you use to make Bogside?' he asked.

'Yeah? So what?'

Henry heaved the machine off its table.

Lamper shouted in panic: 'No! Get your hands off it!'

Henry lifted the machine above his head.

'Don't!' Lamper cried. 'I'll bash your face in! Every day! For eternity!'

Henry hurled the machine down onto the pale

yellow bricks of the bunker floor. It smashed into pieces.

'Noooooo!' Lamper wailed.

Henry turned to Lamper and Bill and announced: 'There'll be no more drugs in Hornet Heaven. We're going clean. It's up to Marco Silva and his team to provide us with ecstasy — in heaven as it is on earth!'

Lamper sobbed: 'I'm not the kingpin any more! Mend it! You've got to mend my machine!'

From across the room, Bill looked at Henry with admiration. Henry had loved Bogside and the rapture-on-tap it had given him. But The Father Of The Club wasn't prepared to accept its downside. Henry was taking a stand and finally doing what Bill had originally wanted to do before the drug had lured him to the dark side. Henry was doing the right thing.

Bill found himself running over to Henry. A few minutes ago, at the 7-1 Southampton game, Bill hadn't been a Watford fan. There had been an empty void at the core of his being. But now he was a Hornet again — and he would be a Hornet for the rest of all time. No dodgy drugs would stop him. Nothing would stop him.

He reached Henry and threw an arm around his old friend's shoulders. His heart was overflowing with Hornet Love. He jumped up and down, crushing the fractured remnants of the Bogside machine beneath his boots. Henry joined in. They bounced together, totally elated.

Eventually Bill and Henry stopped jumping. Lamper was lying on the floor sucking his thumb. The two old men headed out of the bunker, leaving the wreckage of the Hornet Heaven drugs industry behind them.

Henry said: 'Well, that's that, Bill. It's now up to Marco Silva to supply us with our next proper buzz. Let's hope we get a fresh delivery nice and soon.'

* * *

Over the last few days of the international break, Bill and Henry went to watch a number of historic Watford games. They went with other residents who'd experimented with Bogside — including young Derek, the curmudgeonly Frank Gammon, and two fairly recent young arrivals called Ray-Bans and Hipster. No-one took drugs before they went.

All of them enjoyed the old games for what they were — without the need to experience extreme emotion. They had a great time. Already knowing the score took the anxiety out of the occasion — so they could relax and chat with each other. At one match, Ray-Bans and Hipster got everyone to help compile a Top Five of the finest facial hair ever seen on a Watford player. Henry was delighted that his own walrus moustache earned him second place, just behind Marco Cassetti's beard.

Going to the old games particularly helped Frank Gammon. He realised that watching familiar stories unfold helped him manage his anger better. When he watched Watford go 3-0 down at home to Bolton in 1993 he didn't go ballistic because he already knew the ending: a last-minute Gary Porter penalty would win the game 4-3.

Meanwhile, Derek liked the way he could keep an eye out for unusual incidents that happened away from the main action of a match. If he'd been caught up in his own euphoria, he would never have noticed a real-world marriage proposal taking place in The Rookery — just after Troy Deeney completed his hat-trick during the 6-1 win over Bournemouth in 2013. It was a very touching moment — though Derek looked away when the man and the lady started kissing.

At all of the old games, there was so much to enjoy.

None of them wished they'd been tripping on Bogside.

* * *

On the Saturday, Bill and Henry headed off to watch Watford play Southampton again — something they'd done more than 80 times before.

On Occupation Road, Bill said: 'Henry, I want to apologise for how I've behaved during the international break.'

'Goodness me, old chap,' Henry replied. 'Don't blame yourself. In modern football there are all kinds of outside forces deliberately cranking up people's emotions. Fans are manipulated by the broadcasters, the newspapers, the advertisers... Lamper's drug was just another one of those outside forces.'

'But I do still blame myself, Henry. I wish I'd taken a bit more notice of what Malky Mackay used to say when he was manager: "Never too high, never too low".'

'Ah, Malky! One of the game's great philosophers! ...When he wasn't flattening centre-forwards, that is. ...Or sending text messages. But, yes. "Never too high, never too low." Wise words indeed.'

'I know the phrase was intended to apply to

players, but it also applies to fans. Sometimes Watford make me feel great, sometimes they make me feel terrible — but mostly I feel somewhere in between. Especially during the long gaps between matches. I should stay more level-headed. There's no need to hype up my own feelings to try to fill the void.'

'Ah,' Henry said dryly. 'Sounds like you won't be getting yourself a Twitter account any time soon, old son.'

Bill smiled, and the two old friends went through the ancient turnstile to the Southampton game, wondering how they'd feel this time.

* * *

Two hours later, just before the end of the game, as Watford fans anticipated the final whistle against Southampton, Henry said: 'So, Bill. What do you reckon? Exciting enough for you?'

'Definitely,' Bill replied. 'With games like this in Hornet Heaven, there'll never be any need for drugs. Look around at how happy everyone is.'

The real-world crowd was singing a brand new song about Abdoulaye Doucouré.

'Absolutely, old chap,' Henry said. 'We may not be feeling quite as euphoric as we were at the 7-1 win in 1980, but winning 2-0 at St Mary's, to put us fourth in the 2017/18 Premier League will do for me.'

'It'll do for me too, Henry. We've been sensational. This is one of my favourites of the eighty or so games we've played against the Saints. We've won here before, but this feels like a new high.'

'Aha. A high, eh, Bill?' Henry said, cheekily. 'Without it having been narcotically induced?'

'Definitely. Doucouré and Chalobah have been a joy to watch. Marco Silva has got the whole team working for each other. Right now I've got such a warm glow about my club. I must say I'm feeling...

'Go on, Bill. What are you feeling?'

Bill's face relaxed into a huge smile.

He said: 'I'm feeling totally loved up, man.'

THE END

13

DIVIDED LOYALTIES

EARTH SEASON 2017/18

In September 2017, three Watford team-mates from the early 1920s were walking down Occupation Road. Nearly a century on, they were making their way to Watford's latest Premier League away game — at Swansea City.

'You know, I played for Swansea after I left Watford in 1923,' Bert Bellamy said. 'I had some good times there.'

'Ee, listen to you!' Fred Pagnam replied. 'You're a flipping Swan in disguise!'

'Stop teasing him, Paggie,' Skilly Williams said. 'You don't get into Hornet Heaven if you're not 100%

Watford.'

'Quite. Thank you, Skilly,' Bert said. 'To be fair, a small part of me did have a soft spot for Swansea for a while. But in the end I stayed true to my first professional love: wonderful, wonderful Watford.'

'A soft spot for another club? You're a disgrace to Hornet Heaven!' Paggie said. 'When you get through that turnstile, mind you go in the chuffing away section and not the home one!'

Bert, Paggie, and Skilly carried on down the slope and went through the ancient turnstile. They arrived inside the Liberty Stadium.

Bert — known in Hornet Heaven by his nickname Bobbin — led them to join the Watford fans in the upper tier of the North Stand. As the current Watford team took the field, the bald 82-year-old former left-half said: 'Look! Etienne Capoue is in the starting line-up for once.'

White-haired Fred Pagnam, the former centre-forward and manager, said: 'Can't say I care for him, Bobbin. You can tell from Capoue's body language that he doesn't love the club. From the way he plays, I'm not even sure he likes football.'

Flat-capped Skilly, the podgy former goalkeeper,

said: 'Cut Capoue some slack, Paggie. You can't expect every Watford player to love the club. Not these days — what with the loans, the silly money, and all the players from abroad.'

'And you certainly can't insist on them loving the club as much as Troy Deeney does,' Bobbin said. 'He'll be up here in Hornet Heaven when the time comes. No doubt about that.'

'What a load of twod, you two!' Paggie said. 'Every single player should love the club — with all their heart. Otherwise, they shouldn't be playing for us.'

Suddenly a slightly mischievous look came into his eye.

He said: 'I mean, take our game at home to Swansea in 1924. Do you remember it, Skilly? Our team that day included me and you plus Danky Smith, Jock Strain, Eddie Mummery… Virtually everyone in that team loved the club so much that they're now in Hornet Heaven. Oh… Hang about. I don't remember you playing that day, Bobbin.'

'I.. I was left-half, as always,' Bobbin said sheepishly.

Paggie grinned and said: 'And remind me, Bobbin — which side were you playing for?'

'Swansea.'

'Beg pardon, Bobbin? I didn't catch that.'

'Swansea.'

'See? He's a Swan!' Paggie declared. 'Not even in disguise!'

Bobbin turned away. He didn't like feeling his allegiance to the Horns under threat.

Skilly said: 'Leave Bobbin alone, Paggie. He's in Hornet Heaven, not Swan Sanctuary — or whatever they call their place. He's a fully paid-up Horn. Aren't you, Bobbin?... Bobbin?'

Skilly turned to Bobbin. Bobbin was staring into the home fans' section next to them. His face was as white as Swansea's kit.

'Bobbin! Are you alright?' Skilly asked.

'It… It can't be….'

'Don't upset yourself, Bobbin,' Paggie said. 'I were only having a joke. Don't mind me. '

'It's... It's not that.'

'Then what's wrong?'

'I… I… I've just seen *me*. In the Swansea seats. Wearing a Swansea scarf.'

* * *

Bobbin sat with his bald head in his hands. Skilly and Paggie stood and peered into the Swansea seats next to the Watford section.

Skilly lifted his huge flat cap. He scratched his head and said: 'Well, I can't see you in there, Bobbin.'

'I'm sure it was me. Just for a few moments.'

Paggie ran a hand through his white hair, perplexed. He said: 'But how can you have been there? You're dead. If you're here in Hornet Heaven, you can't be in the land of the living as well.'

'I don't know,' Bobbin replied. 'Maybe what I saw wasn't in the land of the living.'

'What? How do you mean?'

'Don't you remember what happened at Christmas last year?' Bobbin explained. 'Our heaven collided with Luton's. Maybe Hornet Heaven momentarily collided with Swan Sanctuary just now — and I saw a glimpse of myself there.'

'But how could you be there and here at the same time?'

'I don't know. Remember I told you a small part of me had a soft spot for Swansea?... Maybe that part of me went to their heaven, while the rest of me came here.'

'Can that happen?' Skilly asked.

'How would I know?' Bobbin replied. 'How would any of us know? But I'm certain it was me. And it means... I'm not 100% Watford.'

Bobbin got up. He wandered slowly back towards to the ancient turnstile with his head bowed, as if he'd lost everything that had ever mattered to him.

Skilly watched Bobbin go. He said: 'We should go with him, Paggie. Make sure he's alright.'

'No. I'm staying. I can't walk out of a Watford match,' Paggie said. He called out: 'Me, I'm a proper Horn, Bobbins.'

'Now you're just being horrible. Especially calling him Bobbins, not Bobbin.'

'Yeah, well, that's because I'm hoping what he were saying were Bobbins.'

Skilly took a closer look at Pagnam. The man who scored 74 goals in 5 seasons for Watford and became the club's third-ever manager was suddenly looking a lot less cocky than he usually did.

Paggie said: 'I mean, if what Bobbin says is correct — you know, that we might exist in other heavens as well as Watford's — it's... well, it's unsettling.'

'Speak for yourself, Paggie,' Skilly replied. 'I was born in Watford, died in Watford and played 341 times for Watford. There isn't a part of me that's not Watford.'

'It's alright for you. I played for four other clubs — so I might be in four other heavens too. I might be in Blackpool's, Liverpool's, Cardiff's and Arsenal's... Oh God!'

'What?'

'Being an Arsenal fan... in 2017... for the rest of eternity... That must be hell.'

'Don't forget you also played for England 14 times. Maybe there's an England football heaven too.'

'Don't be daft! England football heaven? Those three words just don't go together.'

Paggie sat down. He sank his face into his hands and said: 'Being in four heavens puts me in the same boat as Bobbin. I'm not 100% Watford either.'

Skilly Williams lifted his cloth cap and scratched his head again. His old team-mates were in existential crisis. They needed help. And he had no idea where to begin.

* * *

After the Swansea victory, Skilly went to the atrium and found Henry Grover.

Skilly told The Father Of The Club what Bobbin had seen — and explained the theory of players existing in multiple heavens.

'Brilliant! That's just brilliant!' Henry said.

'What?' Skilly replied. 'You think it's good that people up here could be in other heavens too?'

'Absolutely, old thing. I just love the idea that Neil McBain is in Hatter Heaven as well as Hornet Heaven! We can wind him up about that no end!'

'This is serious, Henry. Some of our residents will be very upset. I don't mean the fans — fans only ever support one club, so they're alright. But some of our former players may lose faith in themselves as Hornets. The idea that they're actually spread around various heavens may make them feel like… like…'

'Like tarts?'

'Mercenaries, Henry. The word I was looking for was mercenaries.'

'Oh. Yes. Sorry.'

'So what do you suggest we do?'

'Well, that's easy. Nothing.'

'What? But surely—'

'There's nothing we can do to fix the way the world is. We can't change cosmology. We can't move heaven and earth to—'

'But surely we could find a way to make the players feel better about themselves — couldn't we?'

'What? Oh. Yes. I suppose so. But that would require emotional intelligence, you see, and that's not really my long suit.'

'Then who could help?'

'You'd better go and talk to Bill Mainwood. I think he's in his Man Cave.'

* * *

Skilly hadn't recently visited the shabby red portacabin on Occupation Road. Formerly known as the Bill Mainwood Programme Hut, it was now the Bill Mainwood Man Cave — kitted out with Watford posters, Watford beer mats, and a Watford dartboard.

'Come on in, Skilly.' Bill said.

Hornet Heaven's Head Of Programmes ushered Skilly over to one of the yellow and black striped deck chairs.

'Make yourself comfortable, Bill told Skilly. Then

he called out: 'Derek! Could we have some tea and toast over here?'

'I'm not your slave, sir!' Derek called back.

There was a thud as an angry dart missed the dartboard and pierced the portacabin wall. Bill's 13-year-old assistant, Derek Garston, slouched over to retrieve it.

'Young man! We have a guest in the Man Cave!' Bill said. 'And not just any guest. Skilly Williams made 393 appearances if you include First World War competitions. His son played for us during World War Two. One of his great-grandsons played for us in 1997. He's royalty at our family club.'

'Well, that's a deliberate misuse of club statistics if ever I heard one, sir. First World War competitions don't count. I know what you're trying to do, sir. You're blowing smoke up Mr Williams's —'

'Derek! Are you having a teenage moment, young man? Just bring Skilly his tea. And mind you make it for him in my best mug. The 1977/78 promotion mug.'

Bill and Skilly sat down in the deck chairs. Skilly rested his giant flat cap on his knees and explained to Bill how — after what Bobbin saw at Swansea — Bobbin and Pagnam were feeling unsure that they were actually proper Hornets.

'The thing is,' Skilly said, 'it's not quite as simple for players as it is for fans. Fans only ever have one club, but most players have several. It's not always easy for them to settle on one club as the club they truly love, in their heart of hearts, forever.'

'Golly. I see what you mean,' Bill replied. 'Ever since I was a boy, I've lived in absolute certainty that I'm Watford. There's never been anything else I could be. The idea that I might not be is... Well, just thinking about it would be very upsetting.'

'You *should* think about it, sir,' Derek called out. 'Perhaps, deep down, sir, you're a scummer!'

'I'll ignore that, young man.'

'Anyway,' Skilly continued, 'in Bobbin's case, his job took him to both Watford and Swansea. But he came to our heaven and he's been up here for nearly forty years. In all that time, I've never doubted that he's a Horn. But now he doubts it.'

'I'm not surprised he doubts it, Mr Williams, sir,' Derek said. 'He played loads more games for Swansea than he ever did for us. And he won promotion with them — whereas we stayed in the same division for 35 seasons after he left. Basically, he cheated on us, Mr

Williams, sir.'

'Now, now, my boy,' Bill said. 'It's not fair to see a player as some kind of traitor if he isn't a one-club person like we are as fans. As Skilly says, things are different for players that move around in their careers. They do become emotionally attached to clubs — but for different reasons from us fans, and in ways that are probably quite hard to predict.'

Derek retorted: 'Well, I hope someone works out how to make our new boy Richarlison fall in love with Watford, sir. Apparently he's said he sees us as a stepping stone to greater things at bigger clubs. He's a dirty double-crosser, sir!'

'No, he's not, Derek. He's still young and—'

'But he might become a dirty double-crosser in future, sir. We need to make him love Watford and want to be a Horn forever, sir. And not just him, sir. Prödl... Chalobah... Kabasele... Doucouré. I love them all, sir.'

'Well, maybe you've just hit on the answer, young man,' Bill said. 'Show them you love them. If they feel the love, there's a good chance they'll love Watford back.'

'But if I show them I love them, sir, won't it just hurt more if they do leave?'

Bill sighed. He said: 'Ah, Derek. Sweet, innocent Derek. Of course it will hurt more. But we're football fans. We're already on a collision course with emotional pain — every day of our lives and afterlives.'

Skilly said: 'So, Bill. Do you reckon that's what we should be doing with Bobbin and Pagnam? Showing them how much we love them?'

'Definitely. The only question is how. Let's come up with a plan while we drink our... Derek! Where's that tea?!'

'Right, sir. Think I'm sweet and innocent, do you, sir? Well, you can stick that idea up your—

'Young man!'

'—and your tea along with it!'

The door of the hut slammed behind Derek as he stormed out.

'Derek! Come back here at once! Derek!'

* * *

Some time later, Bert 'Bobbin' Bellamy and Fred Pagnam were in deep gloom behind the Rookery Stand. In the shadowy half-light of that remote part of Hornet Heaven, the two former team-mates were sitting on the wide concrete steps that led down from Stadium Way — the steps that led nowhere.

Bobbin said: 'I keep telling myself I only love Watford — but the thought that I might be in love with another club is gnawing away at me. I'm not an unfaithful man.'

'I was,' Paggie admitted. 'Especially with the women. But when I found meself in Hornet Heaven, I thought I'd settled down.'

'I want to be the kind of person who only loves one club,' Bobbin said. 'I want to have the same exclusive passion as a fan does. But maybe, when you've had a playing career all over the country, you just can't. What do you think, Paggie?'

'Right now, I've no flipping idea. After hearing I might be in four different heavens, I feel like I've totally unravelled.'

Bobbin laid a consoling hand on the bluff Lancastrian's arm. Soon they heard footsteps behind them.

'Oi! You two muppets!'

Bobbin and Paggie turned to see Lamper. The former hooligan — who was now Hornet Heaven's chief steward — was emerging through the murk in his high-vis jacket.

'Someone wants to see you,' Lamper said. 'They told me to tell you that you're "much-loved".'

'Did they?' Bobbin and Paggie asked, simultaneously and hopefully.

'Yeah. That's what they told me to say. I'm not going to, though. I'm going to give you a right pasting — for moping about down here like a couple of miserable gits. Come on! Bring it on! I'll take both of ya!'

'But who was it?' Bobbin asked. 'Who wants to see us?'

'That would be telling.'

'Go on then. Tell us,' Paggie said.

'No way. You'll have to try and beat it out of me. Come on! Come and have a go!'

Bobbin and Paggie stood up and walked past Lamper back towards the eternal sunshine of the upper reaches of Occupation Road. Someone wanted to see them and suddenly they were feeling a lot better about themselves. Maybe they'd lost confidence that they loved Watford, but Watford still seemed to love them.

'I'm not telling you who it was,' Lamper called out after them. 'If you want me to open my mouth, you'll have to kick it open. Come and have a go!'

As Bobbin and Paggie carried on walking away, Lamper sighed in disappointment.

* * *

It hadn't taken long for Skilly Williams and Bill Mainwood to come up with a plan. Now Skilly was standing at the Players' Entrance on Occupation Road. He was holding the door open as dozens of former Watford players passed through into the stadium.

Skilly said: 'In you go, lads. Nice and quick. It's a party in their honour and we want it to be a surprise for them.'

Two of Watford's longest-serving one-club men — Arthur Woodward and Tommy Barnett — filed through in front of Skilly. Behind them was a man who spent many years playing in the top flight for Arsenal, and also represented them in an FA Cup Final, but who was here in Watford's heaven and knew he belonged. The Big Fella nodded approvingly at Skilly.

Behind The Big Fella was someone who wasn't a player. It was a man in a black tracksuit with red and yellow vertical panels on the front; a man who'd been going around making sure everyone knew it was their responsibility to help two Watford players who were having a hard time of it at the moment; a great man; The Great Man.

Skilly watched the last of the players go through the door. He and Bill weren't fully certain that this surprise party they'd arranged in the Players' Family Room — this show of love — would remove all of Bobbin and Paggie's doubts about themselves, but it felt like a good place to start. Suddenly, he heard Derek running down the slope towards him.

'Mr Williams, sir! Mr Williams, sir!'

'Oh. Hello, son. Back again after you stormed off, are you? I hope you're not still in that foul teenage mood.'

'I went to the Swansea game again — to cheer me up, Mr Williams, sir. Richarlison's last-minute goal was just what I needed.'

'Cor! What a moment! I love that boy! I love that team!

'And they loved winning. Did you see the way Richarlison ripped his shirt off in delight, Mr Williams, sir? Though I think he ought to have covered up his nipples, for decency's sake. Tiny, they were, I noticed.'

'I loved the way all the players celebrated at the end. It did my Watford heart good.'

'Mine too, Mr Williams, sir. But the thing is, Mr Williams, sir, when I was there I saw something in the crowd.'

'Really? How do you mean? What was it you saw?'

Derek explained.

Skilly thought for a moment. He looked down Occupation Road and saw Bobbin and Paggie coming up the slope. He said to Derek: 'Quick, lad. Fetch four programmes to the Swansea game. Go!'

* * *

Flat-capped Skilly led the bald Bobbin and the white-haired Paggie through the ancient turnstile, with young Derek in tow.

Bobbin was upset again. He said: 'Lamper said we were much-loved. So why are you taking me back to the Swansea game? You're perfectly aware I'm in a state about which team I support. You wouldn't subject me to this torture if you really loved me.'

Inside Liberty Stadium, Skilly led them all into one of the home fans' areas. They passed through a mass of real-world Swansea fans.

'The home section?' Paggie said. 'If this is some kind of joke you're playing on Bobbin, it's flipping cruel.'

Skilly just said to Derek: 'Show us exactly where to go, boy.'

Skilly, Bobbin and Pagnam followed Derek into the seats in the corner of the North Stand — next to the away fans' section.

Bobbin said: 'Why would you punish me by bringing me back here? This is exactly where I saw myself.'

Then, suddenly, Derek stopped. He pointed.

Bobbin looked.

Derek was pointing at an old man wearing Swansea colours. The old man was sitting quietly, reading a programme, waiting for the game to start.

Bobbin said: 'Why are you pointing at him? What about him?'

'He's the man you saw, Mr Bellamy, sir.'

'What? He doesn't look anything like me. For starters, I saw myself wearing a scarf, not a woollen hat. And I wasn't sitting down. You've made a schoolboy error.'

Skilly looked down at Derek and said: 'I'm disappointed in you, son. You've wasted everyone's time.'

'Stupid blooming kid,' Paggie grumbled. 'Let's get you out of here, Bobbin.'

Bobbin and Pagnam started to leave.

Then, as the Swansea and Watford teams came out onto the field, Derek called out: 'Wait! Mr Bellamy, sir! Look again!

All four of them turned to see the old man stand up to cheer the teams. He took off his woollen hat. Underneath, he was as bald as Bobbin.

'Goodness,' Bobbin said, pleasantly surprised. 'He does look a lot like me. But the person I saw was in the gangway, not at a seat.'

The four men carried on watching as the old man suddenly clutched at his waistband. He whispered to the younger woman next to him, who was also wearing Swansea colours, and started to edge past her.

Paggie said: 'Look, Bobbin! He's going towards the gangway!'

'Oh my goodness! Yes! But wait... I saw myself wearing a scarf. He isn't wearing one.'

As the old man went past the younger woman, she

wrapped her scarf around his neck and patted him on his shoulder.

Bobbin suddenly had tears in his eyes. He said: 'Yes! That is what I saw! It isn't me!'

Bobbin stepped towards Derek and said: 'I'm not a Swan! Not even a part of me!'

Bobbin was so overcome with relief that he lifted Derek up and kissed the boy right on the nose.

'Yuck, Mr Bellamy, sir!' Derek complained. 'That's disgusting!'

Bobbin put Derek back down. Now Paggie lifted Derek up and said with equal relief: 'And I'm not a Gooner!'

Pagnam planted an even bigger, wetter, kiss on Derek's nose.

Derek wiped it off. He said: 'For goodness' sake, Mr Pagnam, sir. I know Mr Mainwood said we should all show love, but this is revolting!'

* * *

Skilly, Bobbin and Paggie emerged from the ancient turnstile onto Occupation Road. They stood chatting while Derek skipped off down the slope.

Paggie said: 'Ee, it feels so good to know for sure that I'm definitely Watford.'

'Me too,' Bobbin agreed. 'Only Watford and always Watford. For eternity.'

'Aye. And not just us,' Paggie added. None of the players up here in Hornet Heaven need doubt their love for this club ever again. We can be as certain as fans are that Watford are our one and only club.'

'And what a time to be a fully committed Watford fan,' Bobbin said. 'This season has started brilliantly. We're only just outside the Champions League places. Just imagine how the season might end.'

Skilly led Bobbin and Paggie towards the Players' Entrance. He said: 'Well, it's good to see you both so happy. When Lamper said you're much-loved in Hornet Heaven, it was true. In fact, we've planned a little surprise party in your honour — to prove it.'

Skilly took them through the Players' Entrance. Immediately on the left was the Players' Family Room. Music was pumping out from behind the closed door — an electro-dance version of Z-Cars.

Skilly continued: 'But I reckon it'll be even more of a celebration now that you've discovered you were definitely 100% Watford all along.'

Skilly opened the door. There was a loud cheer. There was chanting.

'Bob-bin! Bob-bin! Pag-gie! Pag-gie!'

Bobbin and Paggie walked into the party. It was such a simple thing, but hearing their names chanted made them feel totally loved.

They looked around the room. Bill Mainwood was on the decks, dropping the beats. Arthur Woodward was up and dancing — throwing shapes on one of the red and black sofas. The Great Man was chatting away happily in front of one of the huge photos of his great friend Elton John.

Paggie turned to Bobbin and said: 'Look at this, Bobbin. I absolutely bloody love this club.'

Seventy-year-old Paggie launched himself into a few of his best house-music dance moves: stepping left and right, and flinging his feet all over the place. 82-year-old Bobbin joined in. So did Tommy Barnett and The Big Fella. In their enthusiasm, the whole thing ended up looking a bit like a goalmouth scramble without the ball. But they couldn't have been happier.

Skilly made his way over to Bill at the decks. He raised his voice over the music and said: 'You were right, Bill. Love inspires love. All we need to do now is get Watford fans to keep showing love to the current squad — so that players like Richarlison and Doucouré become true Hornets for eternity. You got any ideas on that?'

Bill smiled at Skilly. He said: 'Maybe something like this?'

Bill put on a pair of yellow and black headphones and cued the next track. It was 'September' by Earth, Wind & Fire.

Bill shouted: 'Come on everybody…. 1-2-3-4!'

Everyone chanted: 'Wo-oh-oh, Abdoulaye Doucouré… Never gives the ball away!'

The room resounded. Everyone in Hornet Heaven wanted the flow of Watford players into their afterlife paradise to continue for the rest of eternity — so, for the rest of the night, they all carried on doing their best to make themselves heard down in the land of the living.

THE END

WANT MORE?

This volume contains the stories that were broadcast in Series 3, 4 and 5 of the Hornet Heaven podcast (plus one special out-of-series episode). Future volumes will contain stories from subsequent series and specials.

You can listen to audio versions of the stories by visiting www.HornetHeaven.com or by searching for 'Hornet Heaven' in Apple Podcasts, Google Podcasts, Spotify, or any other good podcasting app.

32502429R00183

Printed in Poland
by Amazon Fulfillment
Poland Sp. z o.o., Wrocław